# LOOKING FOR LOVE

# Looking for Love

## SEVEN UNCOMMON LOVE STORIES

*Edited by Peggy Woodford*

DOUBLEDAY & COMPANY, INC.
GARDEN CITY, NEW YORK

Library of Congress Catalog Card Number 78–19661
ISBN: 0-385-14784-8 Trade
ISBN: 0-385-14785-6 Prebound

# CONTENTS

# LOOKING FOR LOVE

# The Pleaser

## A. L. BARKER

"Marriage is for adults," said the old lady. "Children should live in sin."

"I'm twenty-two!" cried the girl.

"And you still play with dolls."

"Great-grandmama, I collect dolls. I have one of the best collections in the country."

"Age has nothing to do with it. You may not be old enough when you are fifty. Your mother isn't, she has only just reached the giggling stage."

"Great-grandmama, Greg and I are old enough. We are all old enough. And please remember, he is not yet one of the family."

"I speak my mind," said the old lady. "Right or wrong, sense or nonsense, I have not been able to keep anything back. It has made me unpopular. As a girl I was asked to balls, but never to suppers. And I lost men by it. I lost so many that my brother kept a casualty list. They were walking wounded, most of them, hurt in their pride. Eventually I became engaged to a Greek who spoke very little English and by the time he knew enough to realize what I was saying we were married."

"What were you saying?" asked the young man.

"Great-grandfather was a perfect gentleman!"

"One is more likely to be harmed by growing up too early than too late. Twenty-two is about the right age." The old lady said to the girl, "How many men have you had?"

"Oh I say!" said the young man.

"I did warn you," sighed the girl.

"Of course *that* isn't growing up. But people set store by what they call 'sleeping around'—I assume it's a euphemism? In our day we didn't sleep, we were there for the performance."

The young man tugged at his mustache and pulled out several hairs which he could ill afford.

The girl went to telephone her mother. "Great-grandmama is being absolutely prurient!"

"I grew up at fourteen," the old lady went on. "I don't recommend it, it does shorten one's life."

The young man wondered how much longer she was planning to live. He judged she must be about a hundred.

"Ours was a small establishment, my father was a widower and there cannot be a family without a mother. When he remarried the situation was not materially changed from the point of view of my brother and myself."

The young man, straining his ears, thought that the girl talking on the telephone had said, "Great-grandmama is eating arrowroot for Lent."

"She was just four years older than I was," said the old lady, "nineteen, and as pretty as a picture. Who was the man who always painted women with wolfhounds?"

"Landseer?"

"I remember coming home from boarding school and my brother said, 'Who is that lady?' 'That is my wife,' said my father and the matter was not referred to again."

The young man, who was to have a fuss wedding, envied the old lady's father.

"But Caroline hadn't the figure for wolfhounds. She was rounded, what you would call sexy."

The young man wondered if he would. He liked his girls to be slim and piquant.

"She was a tenderhearted creature who wept if a moth flew into the lamp. I thought her foolish. She fostered the impression and I became so concerned for her that I sought to cushion her from the blows of life. I felt—I was very young and of course she was not foolish—that one of the blows life had dealt her was my father.

"You must understand I had had little experience of love, even the sedate filial sort. Our father regarded us as extensions of himself, minor ones, like pimples. He set a rigorous standard, he was constitutionally a rigorous man, and my brother and I were unable to live up to it. But we were obliged to live under it, which was just as constricting. If we offended he said, 'Have the goodness not to do that.' Of course it wasn't virtue he required of us, it was conformity."

The young man distinctly heard his girl say over the telephone, "I can always tell when Greg is shocked, his nostrils open wide."

"And this foolish creature had bound herself to him in ignorance and error. Or could it have been of necessity, I asked myself. What choice did she have? I wasn't sure how many men were like my father. For all I knew he might be the rule rather than the exception.

"I asked her why she had married him. I meant why did she think she was marrying him, what for. The idea of money as a motive did not occur to me. 'Why shouldn't I?' said Caroline. 'Why shouldn't I marry your father?' 'I can give you lots of reasons why you shouldn't,' I said, 'but I don't know one why you should.' 'I love him,' she said, 'that's the one, Miss Nosy. You wouldn't understand.' 'No, I wouldn't,' I said, 'but don't think he can love you. He isn't that sort of man. I shouldn't like you to keep hoping and hoping for—well, you know.' Romance I meant, passion, tenderness, of which I had taken a strong notion from novelettes and ladies' journals.

"Caroline laughed. She didn't have the prettiest laugh in the world. It was too loud."

The old lady removed several rings, including a large diamond, from her fingers and dropped them into an Oxo tin. "Young as I was, I knew when she laughed that she was not quite a lady."

She held up her hand, moving the fingers as if she were waving a flippant goodbye. "Time for my exercises. Why do you want to get married?"

"I want to *be* married and get on with living."

"You are a family man?"

"I'm a Company man. My firm prefers its executive staff to be married."

"How am I to get her off the subject?" the girl was saying into the telephone. "It's the subject we've come about!"

"The poor child," said the old lady.

"She's the only one I could face it with—marriage, I mean."

"Then you must be kind. She was born a woman as all women are, up to a certain point. The fact that she has not progressed beyond that point is not her fault, nor yet her mother's. It is simply bad luck. But are you ready and able to take her on?"

"Yes, I think so—no, I know so. Absolutely. I am to get a fifteen per cent raise—that's automatic on marriage—and I'm next in line for a provincial managership."

The old lady waved her fingers at him. "To take her on beyond that certain point until she is all woman?"

The young man observed that nobody was the same all through, like a stick of rock.

"Bonbons."

"I beg your pardon?"

"It is a closer analogy. Bonbons are sweetmeats," said the old lady. "They may be hard or soft at the center. My father had a soft center, a fact which he had successfully concealed from my brother and I. The atmosphere in our house was sober, not to say somber. Father had the faculty of annihilating all conversation. If one made a remark it either dropped into limbo or was analyzed and reduced to shreds. Caroline's remarks, of which there was a positive flow, were nailed down, even the most idle ones, and scrupulously dissected. I think that in her case it wasn't criticism so much as a hopeless desire to know and be in on everything that concerned her.

"Left to ourselves, my brother and I ran wild in a joyless way. My brother had friends among the village boys and I was often alone. After Caroline came I attached myself to her while my father was away at his office. I had ample opportunity of watching the decline in her spirits.

"She had been a shop assistant, living in one room with another girl, and at first she was happy with the house and grounds and the presents which my father lavished on her —a gramophone, a Persian kitten, jewelry, furs, a ball dress copied from one of Princess Victoria's, a fitted traveling case, five hundred engraved visiting cards. But soon she began to ask, 'When shall I wear my ball dress if there are no balls to go to? Or use my traveling case when I don't travel? What shall I do with five hundred visiting cards when nobody visits us?' 'They're for you to leave when you go visiting,' I told her. 'Well, I don't do that either,' she said, pouting.

"She had a very pretty pout and once I found her practicing it before the mirror. 'Brosy says my face is my fortune and I should be careful how I spend it.' 'Brosy?' 'My brother, Ambrose. He's a captain in the Guards.'

"That was when she began to talk about him. He was fighting in South Africa and when a letter came she read it aloud to us. He had been at Bloemfontein and was coming home on sick leave. 'It's really nothing much,' he wrote, 'a few shell splinters in my right knee, but I'll be out and about again in no time. At least, I'll be out, though my leg will be stiff and I shan't be able to get about much. I'm prepared for a boring time on my own—can't help wishing you were nearer.'

" 'Shell splinters?' " said my father.

" 'Do you think he will always have a limp?' " said Caroline.

" 'Bloemfontein was not shelled.' "

" 'Dearest, did I say it was? Indeed, I wish we were not so far away, the poor boy gets so low when he's alone.' "

" 'He is in London, is he not?' " said my father. 'To be appreciably nearer we should have to reside in the immediate submetropolis, an overcrowded and undesirable area.'

" 'There are very nice houses at the Crystal Palace.'

"My father frowned. 'I cannot see how our living in Upper Norwood could benefit your brother's spirits.'

"In the prettiest possible way she asked if she might invite Brosy to stay for a few days. 'The country air would be good for him'—it was an education to see with what a sweet blend of shyness and appeal she took my father's hand—'and except for you, dearest, he is all I have in the world.' When she called my father 'dearest' I never doubted that she meant it: I supposed that at the vow of marriage she had undertaken not to find anyone else more dear. 'And I do so want him to know you.'

"Father opened his mouth and closed it again. His pale cheeks turned mauve and for once he spoke without attempting to demolish what had been said. 'By all means. He shall stay as long as he chooses.'"

The old lady smiled for the first time since the young man had known her, which was about fifteen minutes. With the smile a thousand fine lines cohered and he saw the face of the girl she had been. It was strangely like the face of his own girl. In another time and place he felt he could have fallen in love with it.

"Mind you, I was predisposed in Brosy's favor. It would have been hard not to be. We saw so few people, any caller constituted a visitation, and Caroline was wildly excited at the prospect of his coming. The whole thing was doomed, of course."

"Doomed?"

"I could not bear to live from day to day as those two did."

The girl came back into the room.

"We mustn't keep you from your afternoon nap," she said, making signs of comfort to the young man above the old lady's head.

"There will be time for sleep soon. All the time in the world."

"Great-grandmama, you are not to be morbid—"

"After tea," the old lady said crisply, "when you are gone I shall take a nap. See that they put marrow jam on the tray, and Battenberg cake. And I have not forgotten some sherry trifle left from lunch."

"But Great-grandmama—"

"And mashed banana sandwiches and fresh cream éclairs. I always make a good tea, it is my favorite meal."

"But Great-grandmama—"

"Do go and hurry them, there's a kind child."

The old lady waved the girl out of the room. She went, with a despairing lift of her hands.

"I well remember the day he came. It was raining and my brother and I were betting on the raindrops as they ran down the landing window. We looked out and saw Brosy marching on us in full uniform, all scarlet and gold, his sword at his side. To me it was like a dream. My brother said it was like the circus coming and Caroline said it was like having a birthday every day. None of us knew or thought to ask what Brosy's coming was like to my father.

"The first words I spoke to him were to ask where his luggage was. He took a comb from inside his hat and a razor from his sword belt and said, 'A soldier travels light.'

"He was handsome, but I thought him pale for a soldier. Caroline reminded me that he had been ill. For Brosy I was anxious to make all possible allowances.

"In fact there was only that one to make, all else was to our benefit. Though I should find it hard to convey to you wherein the benefit lay. He was but a nice young man, cheerful, willing, and with time. He gave me, he gave all of us, the time of our lives. He showed my brother how to run and box and break a horse. From being lazy and dissolute my brother became lively and racketing—not such a great improvement, perhaps, from other people's point of view, but just before he died, at the age of eighty, my brother said to me, 'Those were good days, the best days, with Brosy.'

"How our lives were changed! Our house, which had been full of disapproval, became full of laughter. We made so much noise that I half-expected the ceiling to crack or the pictures to fall down. He had such a way with him. Droll. He was the drollest fellow."

The old lady leaned back and closed her eyes. She appeared to be resting, and well she might. The young man looked at his watch. He had been in the house a little over twenty minutes and she had talked from minute one. He would have liked, if not a rest, at least a preamble, not having been prepared to be dunked so thoroughly in the past.

"You probably wouldn't think so." Awake, she glittered at him from the depths of her chair. "We knew how to enjoy ourselves in the days before Sarajevo."

The young man, who had heard people say that nothing was the same after Munich, wondered what would scathe his generation. Or was his generation scatheless—evolution's answer to the infinite capacity for harm?

"There is no quicker way of changing one's life than by falling in love. And I loved Brosy from the moment I saw him between the winning and losing raindrops, marching on our house in his regimentals. From that moment I lived on the other side of my nature. I think we all did. All except Father. He remained like an iceberg in a summer sea. 'Why this levity?' he said when he found us laughing. 'It's not levity, it's Brosy,' said my brother. 'Call him Captain Spicer—Ambrose, if you wish,' said my father. 'The other is neither a name nor an epithet nor a state of mind.'

"But he wanted so much to be with Caroline in everything she did that when he saw us happy together and although he did not trust happiness he tried to enter into our spirit of fun. Brosy and Caroline were kind, they did not try to keep him out, but my brother and I froze at his approach, cast down our eyes and sat on our hands. It was the way we had been brought up. How unkind children are! Are you prepared for that?"

"Excuse me," said the young man, "but you do seem to have a thing about children."

"That is because I remember the events of my childhood

more vividly and precisely than anything that has happened since. Is this the case with all old people? Is it a recompense for being old—or perhaps it is a debt to be paid?"

"I think it is," said the young man. "The case, I mean."

"Brosy put up a swing in the orchard, he diverted the stream so that we had a pool to swim in. He made us a Chinese devil kite which impaled itself on the church steeple and scandalized the village. As children who had never had anything done for them for love we soon learned—at least my brother did—to put Brosy to work for us. My demands were different. I simply wanted all his attention. So did Caroline, who was able to command it. She would draw him aside and put her arm through his in a sisterly way and lead him out of our sight.

"'It's not fair!' I used to cry. 'She's had him all her life.' 'I expect they want to talk about family matters,' said my brother.

"Brosy was good at translating our extravaganzas into substance. The orchard swing was as near as he could get to my wish to fly, and the boy and arrows he made were the practical answer to my brother's longing for a hunting rifle. I think Brosy would have got us a second best to the moon if we had asked for it.

"But did he love us? I couldn't be sure. Anyway, I didn't want him to love us. Just me.

"I only once saw him lose his temper. It was when I had accidentally splashed him with paint. He called me a clumsy little fool and leaped about slapping himself as if he were attacked by hornets. I was so upset I ran away to the coal cellar and cried there. But he sought me out and knelt down in the coal dust to comfort me."

The young man was thinking of the girl—not his girl, but one sufficiently like her—weeping coal black tears, rather delicious on her white Victorian skin. Sufficient for what? At any rate he was quite envious of the soldier who had consoled her.

"One day my father invited a Mr. Kinglake to supper. This man had shares in the de Beers diamond mines and Father said he wished to talk to Brosy about South Africa. 'But dearest,' said Caroline, 'Brosy was only at the war, not down the mines.' 'It is the war Kinglake wishes to talk about,' said my father.

"But when Mr. Kinglake came Brosy was not to be seen. Caroline told them that he was indisposed and unable to leave his room. 'May we not go up to him?' said my father. 'I'm afraid that is out of the question—' Caroline turned to Mr. Kinglake. 'As an experienced traveler you will appreciate that my brother is suffering from an internal disorder which, happily, is uncommon in our climate.' 'Do you mean dysentery?' said my father. Caroline cast down her eyes. 'Dearest, I chose not to use the word at the supper table.'

"Next morning Brosy was up early working on the tree house he was building for us. He appeared to be fully recovered and ate a hearty breakfast. Father said dryly, 'I am sorry you were obliged to miss your supper last evening.' 'So was I,' said Brosy, helping himself to kedgeree. He was always hungry and he was putting on weight, his clothes were beginning to creak at the seams. 'I was sorry to miss talking to Mr. Kinglake.' 'Perhaps,' said my father, 'the war is not a subject you care to discuss?' 'Why not?' cried Brosy. 'It is a subject, the only subject, which I can claim to know more about than most.'

"And then and there," said the old lady, "he told us how our soldiers, under Lord Roberts, had taken Bloemfontein. The way he told it I could have listened forever. It was so pure and simple."

"Pure?"

She leaned forward and as he met her glittering eye the young man was reminded of something about an ancient mariner.

"Glory is pure and death is quite simple. But to my father nothing was simple. We did not ask for history, my brother and I, but he had to question, to dissect. Was he really hoping to get at the truth? 'According to the *Times*,' he said, 'there was no battle for Bloemfontein.' The *Times* indeed!" The old lady laughed angrily.

"My brother muttered, 'Down with the *Times!*' and I was so carried away as to cry, 'Damn the *Times!*' but before my father could begin to dissect *that*, Brosy said, 'When you are fighting for your life, sir, you don't always remember where you are.' 'So it could have been outside the town?' said my father. 'At Abraham's Kraal?' 'Oh, what do the silly names matter?' cried Caroline. 'Mr. Kinglake,' said Brosy, 'wished to hear from a combatant, a fellow who'd been in the thick—wherever that may have been. Now you can tell him, sir, the way I've told you.'

"To us the notion of my father telling Brosy's stories was painfully funny; my brother and I hid our faces in our hands and pretended we were saying grace.

"It was the uniform which finished them," said the old lady. "The uniform finished everything. As it had begun everything. The number of its days, you see, was the number of ours."

"I'm afraid I don't quite—"

"It couldn't last forever. It was only meant to be worn for a few hours."

"An *army* uniform?"

"Ah, but it wasn't. And although Caroline brushed and pressed and stitched it, it was steadily coming to pieces. One night I went down to the kitchen for a drink of water

and found her steaming the creases out of his tunic.
'You're not to tell anyone,' she said, 'let it be our secret,
yours and mine.' I asked why didn't she get the servants to
do it. 'Because he can't spare his uniform during the day.
Besides, the servants wouldn't take the trouble I do.' He
had nothing else to wear, you see. He could never have
gone to the Crystal Palace."

Why not? the young man thought confusedly.

"My brother wanted him to take us but Brosy said no,
there would be too many people. 'Don't you like people?'
my brother asked him. 'A soldier doesn't have to like people,' Brosy said. 'But you like us?' 'We're different,' said
Caroline, 'we're family.' Brosy laughed. 'I'll tell you what
we'll do instead, we'll go to the Bay and picnic on the
beach.'

"The sea was not far from our house and the Bay, as we
called it, was merely a rocky inlet. We often went there.
Brosy had found an old boat and made it seaworthy and
we used to fish from it and row out to the Pillar Rock
where the seabirds nested. You wouldn't think the Bay
idyllic, it was a stony precipitous place and the water was
thick with seaweed. I can smell the weed now, drying in
the sun."

The old lady lifted the fierce pearly bone of her nose as
if to inhale the perfumes of Arabia.

"Brosy said that the seaweed could be made into bread
or chewed like tobacco or boiled and eaten with fried
bacon. The Chinese, he said, used the sea lettuce to cure
fever. He told us about the seabirds and how they rode the
updrafts from the cliffs and dropped shells from on high to
break them and get at the shellfish. He taught us how to
cook mackerel on the beach.

"He always had time, I used to think he had all the time
in the world and all of it was for us. I am agnostic, but if

there were an Eden for me it would be that little gritty beach with the bladderwrack drying in the sun and the clouds of sandflies and the thick brown surf.

"It was the last time we were ever to go there. After that day, wild horses—"

The old lady lay back in her chair and closed her eyes. She seemed to have fallen asleep suddenly, like a baby. The young man, feeling that her sleep should be respected like a baby's, cautiously uncrossed his legs. He was free now to listen for the return of his girl or to go in search of her.

He remained to gaze at the immaculately cracked face in the depths of the armchair and wonder about the compensations of being old. He thought that knowing it all must be one, knowing the answer to such basic questions as which came first, the chicken or the egg, and knowing about the Holy Ghost and a foolproof way to live. Without time to live it? One of his knees cracked and the old lady opened her eyes.

"He used to take his boots off when we got to the beach so that they shouldn't get scratched. The stones cut his feet. I couldn't bear seeing them bleed and I said, 'Why do you think so much of that stupid uniform?' 'Because everyone else does,' he said. 'People love uniforms. Gold lace and brass buttons hide a multitude of sins.' 'You haven't got any sins!' He laughed, then he said seriously, 'When the uniform goes, so must I.' I cried out, 'You must never go!'

"He and I were alone just then; Caroline and my brother were on the other side of the rocks unpacking the picnic. I told him I loved him. 'Like a woman,' I said, 'you know—' and I hoped he did because I didn't really. But I was longing to learn. I went close, I wanted him to touch me and he did, he stroked my hair. 'No, you mustn't,' he said. I caught his hand and kissed it. 'Why mustn't I?' 'Because love won't make you happy.'

"Just then Caroline called. He caught me round the waist and ran down the beach with me under one arm and his boots under the other. I decided he hadn't meant that about love, it had just been something to say to hide his feelings. And his feelings were so obviously of happiness—I thought I could read him like a book!

"It was a wonderful day, the sun shone, a breeze blew from the sea and we heard a mermaid singing in one of the caves. Brosy said it was a mermaid, such a sweet shrill soulless sound. We knew it was really only the sound of water through a fissure in the rock. But he didn't think the sound of water was enough for us. Nothing was enough for us. Not even himself."

The young man had experienced something like that in relation to his own wedding: he feared that there wouldn't be enough of *him* to justify the fuss. He couldn't come up to the expectations of his girl's family, his own family, his best man even.

"He was the only one who thought so." The old lady said bitterly, "He always had to try to be more than he was and to give more than he had."

The young man, thinking of his girl, thought that *she* was worth the fuss.

To the old lady he said gloomily, "I think it's sort of an initiation, the marriage ceremony. To show you how much you've got to take."

"After we'd had our picnic we all lay down on the beach for a rest. I was beside Brosy and Caroline was on his other side. I held his hand and squeezed it. I was shameless, I trembled with ecstasy, in my innocence I believed that every touch of our fingers was a message of love.

"Then my brother sat up crying that he couldn't endure

the sandflies. I said, 'Who cares about a few old flies?' 'A few?' my brother said scornfully, 'Brosy's covered with them! He holds hands with girls and lets the flies eat him alive. Come on, Brosy, I'll race you to the boat.' 'He can't race,' said Caroline, 'he's got a bad leg.' 'He doesn't limp,' said my brother, 'he never has limped. 'Brosy isn't one to make a fuss,' said Caroline. 'Well, what are we going to do? Sit here all afternoon so you can hold hands?' 'We'll have a race,' said Brosy, 'to see who can find a gannet's egg. We'll divide into teams, you two against Caroline and me.' 'I want to be on your side,' I said to Brosy, 'it would be fairer.' 'There are gannets' nests on Pillar Rock,' said my brother. 'I know,' said Brosy, 'and that makes it fair because they don't nest in the Bay and Caroline and I will have farther to search.'

"My brother wanted to know what the prize was to be. 'A visit to the Crystal Palace,' said Caroline. 'But Brosy doesn't want to go there.' 'He will take you if you win,' she said. I see now that they must have been desperate, poor things. By day there we always were, my brother and I, and by night of course there was my father."

"Desperate?"

"In some countries," said the old lady, "the initiation ceremonies are designed to make children into men and women. But not here. You will come out of church with a child on your arm."

"I would like to know what you mean by a woman."

"Aren't I telling you? Of course I didn't want to go to Pillar Rock, I wanted to be with Brosy. 'You can't,' said my brother, 'he's got Caroline and they'll need to go miles to find a gannet's nest. The gannets are all on the Rock. We'll win easily if you put your back into it.' 'What did you mean,' I said to him, 'about Brosy holding hands?'

'Well he was,' said my brother, 'with you and with Caroline.' And he dragged me away down the beach.

I pretended to help him launch the boat but I was hauling back on the rope all the time. Then I unshipped one of the oars and let it drift. My brother was furious. Then, as the boat slipped out of the shallows, I jumped out. The water came to my waist and my dress, which was of white serge, soaked it up like blotting paper. I was as heavy as a wet puppy but I didn't care. I floundered back up the beach and my brother was so angry he pulled away for the Rock on his own.

"I couldn't see Brosy and Caroline anywhere. They had gone off to search for eggs and I intended to follow them. I didn't care about the silly race or the Crystal Palace, I just had to be with Brosy.

"I expected that they would be going up to the headland and I waited to see them emerge from the cover of the rocks. When they did not, I thought they must have been very quick and were out of sight already. So I climbed all the way to the top of the cliff and looked across the headland. They were not to be seen.

"I went back to the beach. I did not call out; it occurred to me that they might have seen me get out of the boat and be hiding. Caroline, I thought, could make Brosy hide from me.

"I hunted among the rocks. Our picnic things were still there, so were Brosy's boots and his uniform tunic. Out at sea, my brother was rowing strenuously for Pillar Rock. The day which had been so perfect had started to go wrong.

"I went to the caves. I was angry with Brosy, with Caroline, with my brother, with God. I was, you see, a thoroughly spoiled child.

"They *were* hiding, I thought. Caroline was keeping him

from me. She had tried to keep him to herself since the day he came, she was selfish and greedy and low, I thought: she had my father to herself and she had absolutely no right to Brosy as well.

"Oh yes, I thought of people as sweets to be shared. I was still a child. But not for much longer.

"At last I found them. They were in the cave where the mermaid had sung. They were on the floor, making love. Another euphemism," said the old lady, "for the act of beasts."

The young man thought he saw a light and was surprised that she hadn't seen it too and kept out of it. It wasn't exactly flattering to be shown up by Freud.

"I don't know how long I stood watching them. I was paralyzed. It was like a nightmare and I knew I was corrupted by having had it. Whether it was dream or reality I could never be the same again. Those two weren't aware of me, they were locked together, scarcely aware of each other.

"But there was I, aware of everything. No detail escaped me and I could hear the mermaid still singing in the depths of the cave. She was soulless and heartless and mindless as well."

"A rotten thing to happen," agreed the young man. "But if you'd analyzed it—"

"I knew what I knew. There was nothing to diminish it and nothing ever has."

"If you'd been objective about it—"

"There's no fool like a young fool," she said, with scorn for him as well as for the child she was. "I found myself running. My legs took me towards the sea, I meant to drown myself and so I would have done if I hadn't seen Brosy's uniform, his tunic folded neatly on a rock, his boots standing beside it.

"I snatched them up. As I did so, the tunic fell open and inside the collar was a label. It bore a name—I don't remember what—and the words 'Theatrical Costumiers.' You could say that the uniform saved my life."

"Ah. It still inspired tender thoughts?"

"Certainly not. I threw it into the sea instead of throwing myself. Then I went home and locked myself in my room. I was sick several times.

"The others didn't return. They stayed at the beach looking for me and for Brosy's uniform. I tied a scarf round my arm and pushed a pencil into the knot, thus contriving a tourniquet which I tightened until the vein in my arm was ready to burst. The pain kept me from thinking about what had happened.

"When I heard the pony trap returning from the station with my father I ran down to him. He must have been startled, it was the first time I had ever run to him, in joy or in trouble.

"I could not wait for him to get into the house, I began at once to tell him about Brosy and Caroline. He said, 'Have the goodness to contain yourself.'"

"I hope you won't misunderstand me," the young man said carefully, "but sex is not exactly a closed book to your great-granddaughter."

"Sex, as you call it," said the old lady, "is neither here nor there when it comes to growing up. You don't suppose it was the performance I witnessed in the cave which ended my childhood? It was my father who did that.

"He made me wait while he changed his shoes and washed his hands. He offered me, very politely, a glass of soda water so that I might join him while he drank his glass of Madeira before dinner. It was only his impregnable coldness that stopped me from screaming.

"At last he asked what I wished to tell him—to what did

he owe the pleasure of my company at that hour? If he had intended to calm me, he was successful. I began to recite, quite stiffly, the events which led to my discovery. It was not until I came to that and said, 'Brosy and Caroline were in the cave—' that I recalled for the first time—children are so self-centered—that Caroline was his wife and that he had shown signs of feeling something for her. I said, 'They were—you know—' But would he? Wouldn't he insist on a statement? I said the first thing that came into my head. 'They were adulterating'—and because it sounded too stately—'as hard as they could go!'

"I saw him flinch. 'Committing adultery,' he said, and I supposed it was the word, my misuse of it, which he couldn't bear.

"'And incest!' I cried in misery and horror.

"He shook his head. 'They are not brother and sister.' 'Not?' I couldn't believe it. 'Captain Spicer is not a captain. He is not a soldier. His name is not Spicer. He is nothing!' I cried and then, to open wide the wound, 'He is her lover!' He looked at me with the painful cracking of his face which was as near as he could get to a smile. 'That at least is positive.' 'You knew?' Again I couldn't believe, he was talking over my head, as he always did. 'You knew—and you let him stay?' 'It was a question of priorities,' he said.

"Brosy departed next day, wearing a pair of the gardener's shoes—the only ones which fitted him—and a Norfolk jacket of my father's. We did not see or hear of him again.

"Caroline had a son who grew to be the image of Brosy but whose disposition was exactly my father's. It was a judgment on us all."

She took her rings from the Oxo tin and replaced them on her hand. 'No more exercises, my fingers are tired."

"Priorities?" said the young man. "You can get those wrong!"

The girl returned, bringing a tray with a bowl and spoon on it. "Great-grandmama, are you ready for your supper?"

"I am ready for my tea. I don't eat supper. Ah, it's *kakavia*."

The girl tied a clean white napkin round the old lady's neck. "Great-grandmama's hands are too stiff to hold a spoon—"

"Fish, onions, tomatoes, celery, lemons, and half a pint of olive oil," said the old lady. "Only the Greeks could think of such a dish."

To the young man the stuff in the bowl looked like chicken soup. He watched as the girl began to spoon it into the old lady's mouth. When a trickle ran down her chin the girl tenderly wiped it away.

"Your young man is shocked," said the old lady. "Look at his nostrils."

"Is the *kakavia* all right, Great-grandmama?"

"Not enough oil in it." The young man couldn't be sure if she winked at him or had a tic in her eyelid. "No one cooks like the Greeks."

When he and the girl were in the train on their way home he said, "Your great-grandmama hasn't had a genuine human relationship since she was fourteen. I suppose it's natural for a young girl to be scared when she sees life coming for her."

"What are you talking about?"

"You know what I think? She was on to a good thing when she saw those two in the cave, and she knew it."

"What two? What cave?"

"I think she wanted an out and that was it. She took it. She let old biological necessity Sex shake her frigid and

she's been in the deep freeze ever since. Freud was right.
Your great-grandmama has never lived."

"Freud? You *were* drawn. I warned you, didn't I?
There's no need to be sorry for Great-grandmama. She's
had a wonderful life."

"In the freezer."

"Darling, she's incredibly old and it's hard to believe,
but it's family history and I would have told you anyway.
In her youth she was a great amoureuse. Freezer?" The
girl laughed with pride and satisfaction. "She was what
you would call a hot number."

"I would not, I detest the term."

"Well, it was altogether a biological necessity with her.
She was the cause of quite a scandal in the Army."

"The Army?"

The girl twinkled at him. "Great-grandmama was always partial to soldiers and she had so many affairs that her
brother was obliged to resign his commission. After that,
she married a middle-aged Greek. Everyone was staggered.
But enough was enough, and she knew it. They were won-
derfully happy. She adored him and he spoiled her utterly.
Greeks are like that."

"Like what?"

"Awfully uxorious."

"Why did she tell me that story?"

"She loves to tell stories."

"Things don't just happen," the young man said firmly.
"They're relevant. I believe that. She told me a story and
there was something in it for me. I should know—I *must*
know—what it was."

The girl put her head on his shoulder. He sat frowning
in thought. The motion of the train made the girl drowsy
and she fell asleep.

Presently he asked, "Do you know any Greek girls?" but she did not hear. He gazed into her face: she did not look like her great-grandmama at all. He kissed her and went to sleep.

# A Surplus of Lettuces

## EMMA SMITH

"The Kendalls are back, Mum," said Elsie Parr to her mother one Thursday afternoon. They were cleaning the shop out, unhurriedly, as they did every half day, more by way of an occupation than because it was really necessary; what other occupation was there on a Thursday afternoon? "I ran into Dick Kendall down at the petrol pumps when I went for the bread, dinnertime. You should have seen the car he was driving—bright yellow, the color of our canary. It was his dad's car, he said, not his. He didn't know who I was till I spoke. But I knew him, straight off."

"The Kendalls back—in Bingley? Never!" exclaimed Mrs. Parr. Anything that happened in a village the size of Bingley—and nothing much ever did happen—was immediately common knowledge.

When Elsie replied that the Kendalls had rented a furnished house for the summer over at Croxham, her mother was mildly reproachful: why had she failed to mention it before? Her father could have had it as an interest to turn over in his mind while he was struggling to trench the potatoes. Supplying Mr. Parr with items of news was the self-imposed duty of his wife and daughter;

news, usually so hard to come by, helped to keep him from brooding too much on his handicap.

Mr. Parr had only one arm. He had lost the other in an accident when Elsie was three. In those days he worked for the railway and Elsie had a memory of the station as it used to be then, and of being lifted by her father in both his arms and held in both his arms and held high to watch the goods trucks go clanking through. No trains, goods or passenger, passed through Bingley today. Bingley had lost its station shortly after Mr. Parr lost his arm. The branch line had been closed, and the rails torn out; where they had once glittered—as Elsie remembered it, dangerously—grass now grew.

With the accident compensation money Mr. and Mrs. Parr set up business in a sweet-and-tobacconist shop. It sold a conglomeration of other articles too—pencils and India rubbers and ink and picture postcards, and Mrs. Parr kept a drawer stocked with cotton reels and elastic; orders were taken for newspapers and magazines. Judged even by Bingley standards the shop was a modest little shop, but the Parrs were modest people. Their ambition was to manage somehow, and somehow for thirteen years they had managed. In the small garden behind the shop Mr. Parr contrived to grow enough vegetables to provide for the three of them. Occasionally there was a surplus. Then a notice would be propped on the pavement outside the shop: *Lettuces for Sale.*

Mrs. Parr was much struck by the coincidence of Elsie happening to pass Ron Foster's garage just as young Dick Kendall was drawing up for petrol. "If you'd have gone for the bread earlier, Elsie, like you meant to do, you'd have missed him."

But Elsie continued to polish away at the counter industriously without answering her mother. The coincidence appeared to her to be less crucial. She had no doubt that since the Kendalls were back in the district she was bound to have seen them sooner or later. Elsie had been waiting a long time for the Kendalls to come back. In her heart she had been expecting them, constantly, for years.

When the Kendalls first came to Bingley she had been eight, the same age as the youngest of the four Kendall children, Louisa. An elderly retired admiral and his wife had lived at the Old Rectory before the Kendalls took it over, and in their day the big white gate at the end of the gravel drive had been kept always discreetly closed. After the Kendalls came it was always open. The Kendalls had a habit of not shutting gates or doors or windows, ever.

Louisa and Elsie attended the same primary school in Croxham, six miles off. The Old Rectory, as well as being the largest house in Bingley, was the first, and the sweet shop was situated conveniently close to it, not more than a hundred yards or so farther along the street from its drive-way entrance. On countless frosty, rainy, foggy, sunny mornings the two little girls had waited together by the big white gate for the school bus to pick them up. In class their desks were set next to one another's, and nearly every day of the week when school was over Elsie had had tea at the Old Rectory and stayed on to supper. It was Louisa who invented the secrets they whispered, the games they played, and Elsie, respectful of her friend's inventive genius, had been content that she should; only, she would have been glad to have played each of the games for longer—Louisa liked to change her games often. And there was one game that Elsie sometimes did refuse to play:

"Let's go down to your shop and get some sweeties."

"No."

"Why not?"

"I don't want to."

Sometimes, however, Elsie agreed, reluctantly, and they went, and then Mrs. Parr would let them have triangular paperbags filled with lemon sherbets and glacier mints. "My goodness, but she's a chatterbox, the Kendalls' youngest," Mrs. Parr used afterwards to comment to her husband. "She doesn't allow that tongue of hers to lie idle a second. It's a blessing our Elsie hasn't much to say for herself."

Mr. Kendall worked mostly at home. He was a writer; he wrote popular historical novels, two of which had been filmed. In between writing novels he rewrote the autobiographies of famous people, making them less stodgy to read and more amusing. His wife's hobby was sculpting in clay, a hobby that saved her, she frankly admitted, from the chores of housework and cooking—and saved her family, she would add, laughing, from a diet entirely of omelettes! Mrs. Jellicoe, the chimney sweep's widow, came in daily to clean and bake, and it was Mrs. Jellicoe's sharp eyes and ears that provided the village with material for gossip. The gossip varied: according to one tale, the Kendalls were fabulously rich; according to another, they were undischarged bankrupts. For Bingley was at a loss to know what to make of these bizarre migrants, and the migrants themselves, living blithely apart on the outskirts of Bingley, were totally unconcerned as to what its inhabitants might or might not be making of them.

Because of their daughter's association with the Kendall family, Mr. and Mrs. Parr would have no part in the gossip. During term time Elsie practically lived round at the Old Rectory. It was different, of course, in the holidays when the two Kendall boys and Louisa's older sister, Natalie, came flocking home from boarding school, as likely as not bringing friends with them. All day long, then, shouts and laughter resounded from the other side of the high brick wall, and Elsie stayed away. Mrs. Parr was at liberty to get on with her fruit preserving in the kitchen. Elsie minded the shop. For hours and hours, trade being generally slack, she would sit on a stool like a grown-up person, knitting, and if any of the Kendalls looked in to buy a bottle of squash they were greatly amused to be served by Elsie. They teased her, quite without malice—the Kendalls were very good-humored—and then they would race off again with their bottle of squash, never thinking of suggesting to Elsie Parr that she should come with them.

At seven o'clock every morning Elsie delivered the newspapers to the Old Rectory, but at that hour she saw no one; it was too early for the Kendall household to be astir. When Mrs. Parr reckoned Elsie had knitted enough for a child of her age, she used to concoct errands to send her on. Elsie would be given a pot of new jam and a message for Mrs. Kendall, or perhaps a couple of Mr. Parr's lettuces to help out—she was instructed to say—with their houseful of visitors. The Kendalls themselves grew no lettuces; they grew groundsel instead. They mowed the lawn assiduously so as to be able to play cricket on it, and rounders, but that was the only gardening they ever did. By the end of their third year at the Old Rectory the Admiral's careful garden had become a wilderness, a riot of roses in a flourishing tangle of weeds.

Ah! but a wilderness was beautiful, Mr. and Mrs. Kendall would assert, much more beautiful than clipped hedges and herbaceous borders. And the children said the same: a jungle was much more fun, they said—neat gardens were so boring. Elsie withheld this opinion from her father, who cultivated his own limited plot of ground with extreme neatness. Undeniably, though, Mr. Parr's vegetable garden was not a place in which to have fun. Elsie, too, thought a wilderness beautiful. Nor did it occur to her that had the

Kendalls stayed on for another year or two the jungle would have overtaken the garden completely, and the huge velvety cabbage roses reverted to briars, and the delphiniums and hollyhocks, planted by a previous owner, been choked to death.

Elsie was never quite sure when she arrived on her own at the Old Rectory, armed with the lettuces or the pot of jam but without Louisa for escort, which door would be the right one for her to go to; and ought she to walk into the house boldly, as she was accustomed to doing with Louisa, or ought she to ring the bell? But somebody, while she was hesitating, would inevitably catch sight of her, would hail her: "Elsie! It's Elsie Parr!" And then it was easy for her to attach herself to the game of cricket: an extra fielder was always welcome. When Elsie was eleven the Kendalls left Bingley.

She had been in love with them for eight years—for the three years they had lived in the village, and the five since they had gone: half of her lifetime. She had been in love, and she still was, with Mr. Kendall and Mrs. Kendall and with Adrian and Natalie, the two eldest children, and with Dick, who was fourteen when they went, and with Louisa. She was in love, still, with their cats and their dog and their guinea pigs and their white mice and their parrot, who must all be dead by now. Inside her head for years she had kept them secretly alive. Elsie was like her father, reserved; she concealed her emotions. Nobody guessed that inside her head the Kendalls ran and leaped and whistled and sang. She saw them, bursting out of doors; she heard them, shouting from windows. One day—she had been certain of it—they would come back. And now they had.

But when Mrs. Parr learned that her daughter intended to bicycle over to Croxham on Sunday so as to renew acquaintance with their former neighbors, instead of encouraging Elsie she shook her head and advised against it. Elsie was surprised by this attitude: she had expected support from her mother. She was also perplexed. For in spite of Louisa Kendall's disappointing record as a correspondent—one Christmas card meagerly fulfilling her lavish promises to write—she had once been Elsie's best friend.

"Maybe so," replied Mrs. Parr, "but if she wants to see you, Elsie, she knows where to find you. There's no need for you to go chasing after her. I wouldn't want Mr. and Mrs. Kendall to think you were pushing yourself at them, just because they lived next door to us all those years ago and were good to you when you were little. It's not the same now, Elsie. You leave things be."

Elsie rolled her polishing cloth into a tight ball and squeezed it between the palms of her hands. How could she leave things be? If she did nothing, then nothing would ever change. A shiver of panic went through her, a curious terror that it was going to be Thursday afternoon in Bingley for the rest of her life: the blind at the door lowered; the ribbons on the dummy display boxes of chocolates faded; the street outside, hot with sunshine, empty. And she remembered a rhyme made up by Dick Kendall which he and the others used to chant often and loudly, in glee at its wittiness:

> "Elsie Parr
> Won't go far.
> Ha ha ha!
> Elsie Parr."

She had been a good child, so willing and tractable that people had called her old-fashioned. Her mother seldom had to scold Elsie; her father had never chastised her. Trained up to be obedient to her parents as they, in turn, were obedient to the confining circumstances of their existence, Elsie resembled them. "Anyone can tell whose daughter you are!"—how frequently she had had it said to her. In Mr. and Mrs. Parr's fond estimation she was a copy of themselves, a younger version, and she until recently had thought as they did. But in the last few weeks Elsie, vaguely restless, had begun to wonder whether she might not be like someone else: like Elsie Parr, in fact. A new Elsie Parr, who was sixteen and very pretty, as Dick Kendall down by the petrol pumps had instantly perceived even though her own mother and father had somehow failed to do so.

"He asked me to go over, Mum. He invited me."

Dick Kendall's actual words, uttered in the light bantering manner characteristic of all the Kendalls, were: "Nice to have seen you, Elsie Parr. See you again, perhaps, one of these days." But his eyes had admired her, and that was her invitation. Her mother had said it was not the same now—and indeed, it was not! For now she had something better than lettuces to bring them, to lay at their feet like a tribute: this gift of her prettiness.

"You go, then," said Mrs. Parr, "if you've set your mind on it."

Elsie started out on her bicycle for Croxham the following Sunday morning as soon as she had finished washing the breakfast dishes. The weather was appropriate to a Kendall expedition; the sun shone in a wide blue sky and a summery wind was blowing the scent of honeysuckle in gusts from the hedges. Pushing her bike up the long slope of Baggotts Hill she remembered how, in Julys gone by, she and Louisa used to lie on their stomachs in the grass making daisy chains to hang round the necks of the Kendall guinea pigs. She remembered their swing, and how enticingly it had dangled from a bough in the sun-speckled shade of the great chestnut tree. And then, at the top of the hill as she paused with a foot on the pedal preparatory to mounting and coasting off down the farther side, another memory of the Old Rectory garden in summertime hit her like a stone dropped from the cloudless heaven above. How could she have forgotten it?

How could she have forgotten the blur of strange faces turned towards her one hot afternoon?—staring as though it were she who was the stranger; as though she had been an intruder. Again, shamingly, she heard Mrs. Kendall's clear voice: "Oh, Louisa—you shouldn't have asked Elsie to tea today, darling—not *today*"; and Louisa's indignant reply: "I didn't ask her, Mummy." Again she was standing at the corner of the house, rooted, clutching her jar of home-bottled gooseberries, unable to move a step forwards or backwards; and again Louisa was running across the lawn to her. "You can't come today, Elsie—we've got friends." It had been the wrong day for Elsie to have ventured by herself down the gravel drive of the Old Rectory.

Elsie laid her bicycle in the ditch. For more than a quarter of an hour she sat on a field gate and wondered which direction to go in: Bingley or Croxham? Then she picked up her bike and pedaled slowly on to Croxham. And even though it was a Sunday morning, all the way there, absurdly, she dreaded to find them grouped about a tea table, as then, on a lawn identical to the Old Rectory lawn at Bingley. Suppose it were to be the wrong day again?

Croxham was a considerably larger village than Bingley. When she reached it, the church bells were ringing and the shops were shut. Presently, however, she came on a small general store that was open, and she propped her bike against the curb and went inside, thinking that very probably the shopkeeper would be able to tell her the Kendalls' address. There was a customer in the shop already, a woman buying coffee and biscuits. Her back was turned, and Elsie was blinded as well by the gloom of the shop's interior coming after the glare outside. Nevertheless she knew immediately who it was: that crystal-clear indulgently laughing voice was unmistakable. And it flashed upon her then that no other voice had ever called her *Elsie darling*. Her mother's more humdrum term was *Elsie dear*.

Mrs. Kendall paid for her shopping and went past Elsie with a glance and a smile; the friendly noncommittal smile she gave so freely to all the world. "Oh, Mrs. Kendall," said Elsie, and Mrs. Kendall stopped. "You won't remember me, I don't suppose. I'm Elsie Parr, from Bingley."

"Why Elsie!—How you've altered! You've quite grown up! And my goodness, aren't you lovely!" Taken aback by the uninhibited warmth of the greeting, Elsie flushed pinker with pleasure, and her eyes began to sparkle.

Mrs. Kendall herself had not altered, except perhaps that she looked a great deal younger than Elsie's own mother. Her figure was slender and her short curly brown rumpled hair, which both of the boys had inherited, was untouched by gray. With a most gratifying assumption of familiarity they strolled off side by side along the village street, Elsie pushing her bicycle and Mrs. Kendall chatting away as easily as though she and Elsie were the same age—twenty-five —and it was they who had once been to school together. She told Elsie the family news, referring to her husband as Neil.

Adrian, it seemed, was married, and Natalie was at art school, and the rest of them had been in America for the last two years where Neil had had a terrific success. Americans, Mrs. Kendall confided to Elsie with mockery and approval, always went crazy over Neil—they thought him so English. The States had been a marvelous experience, but now, she said, Dick had to be settled into an English university, and Louisa had to prepare for her A-level exams, and none of them wanted to turn absolutely Yankee, so here they were, home again, having rented this perfectly horrible brand-new bungalow—not a bit their style—for a couple of months as a stopgap while they were sorting themselves out and deciding on the next move.

"I wish you'd come back to Bingley," said Elsie, made fully confident by Mrs. Kendall's kindness.

"Oh, wasn't it bliss!" agreed Mrs. Kendall.

In Croxham, as in Bingley, the Kendalls were living on the fringe of the village. The bungalow that Mrs. Kendall had described as perfectly horrible looked to Elsie as though it might have been built for a film star; she had seen illustrations of similar bungalows in magazines. "I believe it won a prize—imagine!" Mrs. Kendall exclaimed with offhanded amusement.

Elsie's top-of-the-hill memory vanished into the sunny air like a childhood nightmare, gone on waking. The Kendalls were so obviously glad to see her. Apparently Dick had not mentioned Thursday's encounter. This to Elsie was understandable. But what she attributed to reticence—she was reticent herself—in fact was due more simply to her having passed clean out of Dick Kendall's mind the moment he trod on the accelerator of the yellow car. All of them, though, were genuinely pleased by her surprise arrival on a Sunday morning otherwise rather blank.

Louisa gave a shriek of joy when she learned who it was that her mother had picked up, shopping. Natalie, the sophisticated Kendall, leaned from a window to call hullo, and Mr. Kendall behaved as if Elsie had never been less important and interesting than a pretty girl of sixteen. Only Adrian was absent; he and his wife were to drive down from London to Croxham that afternoon.

They sat and lay and sprawled in the garden round a tray of the coffee and biscuits Mrs. Kendall had been buying, informal, friendly, not in the least condescending. Do you remember? they said. Surrounded by Kendalls, all smiling at her, Elsie was completely happy.

"Do you remember how we ambushed the postman?"

"And Adrian's bombs?"

What *bombs?* Mrs. Kendall, mystified and retrospectively alarmed, had to be enlightened by Dick: the bombs had consisted of brown paperbags crammed full of grass cuttings and damped so as to make them burst on impact. "They were brilliant—"

"Oh, weren't they?—Adrian ought to have patented them."

"And what about the day we played firemen— remember? And you soaked Mrs. Jellicoe, Dick, with the hose, and Elsie was locked in the linen room, screaming the house down—she thought she was going to be roasted alive—"

"You never knew when it was real, Elsie, and when it was just a game," they told her affectionately.

Time, she believed, had closed the gap, had magically equalized them. Sixteen and pretty, she qualified now, at last, for membership in the Kendall Club, could look back as one of them at the quaint and solemn little figure that had been herself and borrow their laughter.

"You were so polite, Elsie—"

"And we were so rude!"

"You were always bringing us lettuces and we hated lettuces. Daddy said you must have thought we lived in the Old Rabbit Hutch, not the Old Rectory." Louisa doubled up with mirth at her father's long-ago joke.

"It was very considerate of Elsie's mother." From the corner of an eye Elsie glimpsed Mrs. Kendall shake her head at Louisa, and frown. A wisp of cloud crossed the sun, cast its faint shadow; evaporated.

"They were Dad's lettuces," she said quickly, laughing too, to show that it was all right to laugh. "It's him does the garden, not Mum."

Mrs. Kendall inquired after Elsie's father. Besides growing vegetables on his patch of ground Mr. Parr was Bingley's accredited odd-job man. He did house decorating and chimneysweeping. In the past the Kendalls had sent for him when they needed to have their drains unblocked or when winter gales blew slates off the roof of the Old Rectory.

"He was a nice chap, your father." Mr. Kendall spoke through the meshes of his wife's straw hat with which he had covered his face as he lay stretched out comfortably on the lawn. "A very dependable chap, I remember. Whatever he did, he did it exceedingly well." Neil Kendall enjoyed being generous in his praise of others. He liked to like people, even as he liked to be liked—it was a fair exchange; all the Kendalls possessed a strongly developed sense of fairness. Americans in Hollywood had considered him typical of the very best sort of an Englishman, the sort who gave himself no airs and was as much at his ease with the chap who unstopped drains as with the grand old Duke of York.

"Dad misses the engines, I think," said Elsie. It occurred to her here in Croxham, with the advantage of a six-mile perspective, that he had been missing his engines as she had missed the Kendalls, for years.

"Then he ought to get himself a job again with British Rail."

"Oh, Neil!" protested Mrs. Kendall. "It's not as easy as that—he must have tried, poor man."

"Perhaps he hasn't tried hard enough," suggested Mr. Kendall.

Elsie was silent; she had a sudden picture of her father,

with his artificial arm strapped on for the purpose, dog-
gedly trenching potatoes in the small garden behind the
shop. And it came to her, not precisely in words but on a
wave of inarticulate feeling, that all his powers of trying
hard had been used up in the long struggle to survive.

"Father believes that you can get anything you want in
the world," explained Natalie, "if you only want it badly
enough—don't you, Fa?"

"Well, of course I do," he maintained with a boyish bra-
vado from under the straw hat. "Of course you can!—I've
proved it myself, haven't I?"

His family shouted at him, and jeered, and laughed in
the delight of knowing, as he did, that what was true for a
Kendall was by no means necessarily true for anyone else.
Kendalls were a special breed, beloved by the gods; Kendalls were lucky.

Mrs. Kendall asked Elsie how Bingley was getting along
these days. It was a question not intended to be taken too
seriously. When Elsie embarked on a saga of marriages,
births and deaths, she could feel their interest ebb. She was
talking of people unknown to them. Ernie Ogden they
knew because he had delivered their milk every day, and
Mrs. Jellicoe they knew because she had cleaned their
house. Bingley was bounded for the Kendalls by the high
brick wall of the Old Rectory. Nor, really, did they want
to hear anything about the place as it existed now: Bingley
was the Old Rectory when *they* had lived there.

Somebody mentioned school and Louisa brightened. Did
Elsie remember when she, Louisa, had cheeked the driver
of the school bus, and he had halted the bus and ordered
her to get down, and she had, and it had been snowing, and
there was a terrible row about it later on? Yes, Elsie
remembered this episode. And yes, she remembered the ge-
ography teacher's habit of mopping his brow with the

blackboard duster, and the headmaster's green braces, and the name and separate identity of every boy and girl in their class. Louisa was an entertaining raconteur. Her family applauded her. And yet she seemed to Elsie oddly childish—almost, Elsie without disloyalty reflected, babyish —for sixteen. It was puzzling because at nine and ten she had been counted old for her age: precocious.

Louisa, shaking back her curtain of blond hair, bewailed the fate that condemned her to suffer two more whole years of beastly school while Elsie was already free as air.

"What will you do, Elsie, now you've left school?"

Elsie said she was helping her mother in the shop.

"But you can't help your mother in that shop of yours for the rest of your life—it's so tiny, isn't it?"

"And anyway, Bingley's such a dead end of a place—"

Elsie sat happily waiting to be told by the Kendalls what she should do with the rest of her life. She had a vision of the canary-yellow car whisking her away out of Bingley towards some vague and glamorous horizon. Whatever they told her to do, she would do it.

After a pause that lasted for more than half a minute Mrs. Kendall said Elsie must be sure to stay for lunch; it was so nice of her to have bicycled over from Bingley on purpose to see them. Dick yawned. Louisa wanted to know if there was ice cream for pudding again today; she was sick of ice cream, she said.

Lunch began somberly, unrelieved by conversation. The lively breeze of reminiscence having blown itself out, the mood had changed. Everyone retreated behind a barricade of private thoughts, although Mrs. Kendall at least, in her capacity of hostess, did occasionally speak to Elsie, absent-mindedly asking her if she would like another helping of beans or a glass of water. Hoping anxiously to revive their laughter, Elsie reminded them of Dick's rhyme: "Elsie Parr, Won't go far—"

Louisa glanced up from her plate. "Well, and he was right, wasn't he?—you haven't gone far." Her tone was cheerfully final. It consigned Elsie Parr to Bingley forever.

Elsie, in the midst of them as she had so often dreamed of being, was alone. They had forgotten her again. Once, one wet afternoon of the summer holidays playing hide-and-seek at the Old Rectory, Elsie had hidden in the attic, in a cupboard. When she emerged from the cupboard the rain had stopped and the house was deserted: on a sudden impulse Mr. Kendall had bundled his family into the car and driven them all off to the seaside.

With a sinking heart, but forcing her voice to imitate a Kendall airiness, Elsie addressed herself to Dick. "Why was it you called your parrot Tiger Tim, Dick?—I always wondered." And indeed it had been one of the enigmas of her childhood.

"Oh, that moth-eaten old creature—Neil christened it. Didn't you, Neil?" he bawled at his father, carelessly, down the table. Mr. Kendall took no notice of him. Mumbling from impatience to be rid of an explanation that bored him, Dick told Elsie it was to commemorate some antediluvian children's comic published in his father's youth.

"But a parrot's a bird," she persisted, nervously jaunty. "It seems so funny to call it a tiger."

Neither Dick nor Louisa answered her. They looked at each other, though: the merest flicker of a look.

"Tiger Tim was the *name*, Elsie, of a children's comic," murmured Mrs. Kendall softly, as if Elsie had shown something she should not have shown. "And there was a parrot, you see, *in* the comic."

Natalie said, speaking without preface from the pool of

their shared private thoughts: "I can't think why on earth we don't decide to have a flat in Paris, and be done with it."

"Because your mother, Nat, has this bee in her bonnet about the glories of the Italian countryside and treading her own grapes, or some such nonsense. Personally, I prefer London."

"No, you don't, Neil—you're yearning to set up as an Englishman in Boston, Massachusetts, or Washington, D.C."

"Oh, for heaven's sake, let's leave it—can't we?—till Adrian's here—"

They resumed the internecine wrangle that Elsie's arrival had interrupted a few hours earlier. With a sense of profoundest shock she realized that what she had thought of as a reunion had been a visit, and the visit was over. She should have departed before now. Nobody told her to go; they simply behaved as though she had gone already.

What was Bingley to the Kendalls but a fragment of their past for which they felt, since it was theirs, a certain tenderness, an intermittent nostalgia? And Elsie Parr was a fragment of Bingley. It was not for Elsie's sake they had crowded round her when she first arrived, but because she brought them snapshots of themselves, and old photographs are always amusing to look at, and exclaim at, for a while; after a while they cease to be amusing. The present has a stronger hold, and the future is more alluring.

Elsie stayed on and on. How was she to tear herself away? When she went it would be ended, she knew: she would never see them again. Who then was she to love, and wait and hope and long for? Who but the Kendalls could open a door for her into the enormous world beyond? It would be Thursday afternoon in Bingley with no trains passing through, forever.

She made herself useful. She washed up the lunch dishes. "Oh Elsie, how very sweet of you, darling—I was going to leave them soaking till tomorrow for Mrs. Thingummy to do." She sat in the garden pretending to read the Sunday newspapers, reassembled from a disorderly mess of pages strewn across the lawn. Dick lay asleep in the shade of one tree; Natalie was busily writing a letter in the shade of another. The rest of the family had dispersed out of sight. Half an hour went by; the telephone rang. Louisa yelled from a window that Adrian was on the line—he wanted to speak to Dick. There was some hitch; he had been delayed. More shouting followed, with voices raised from room to room. Natalie continued coolly to write her letter. When she had finished she borrowed Elsie's bicycle and pedaled off to the village to post it. Elsie resolved that immediately Natalie returned, she would go.

She would go without saying goodbye. It would surprise them, because Elsie Parr had always been so polite. They would remark on it to each other: "Didn't she say goodbye to you? I wonder why not." And perhaps they might wonder, when it was too late, and they had lost her, what Elsie Parr was really like.

Natalie came spinning back on the bicycle, sophistication discarded. A fifteen-year-old schoolgirl again, she was ringing the bell in a frenzy of exaggerated warning and crying out: "Beware! Beware! Take cover! Old Muggins is on the warpath!"

The Kendalls throve on minor crises. They had an aptitude for converting any incident, however slight, into pleasurable drama. Relishing their own dismay they gathered tribally on the lawn.

"Why didn't you head him off, Nat, for God's sake?"

"Why didn't you say we'd got the plague?"

Again, briefly, Elsie was enlisted on the side of the Kendalls. The enemy approaching now was not, as it used to be, the postman or the Vicar from a neighboring parish, but a lifelong friend of Neil Kendall's who lived in Croxham. He was an entomologist, Louisa told Elsie; an entomologist was somebody who was mad on beetles—he collected them and studied them under a microscope and wrote articles about them for the British Museum, or somewhere. Dick, more sweepingly, declared that he was the biggest bore on earth.

"Oh yes, he is, Mother—play fair! You've said it yourself —you know you have—a million times."

Mrs. Kendall admitted that William Murgatroyd was a little dull. "But he's a dear old thing, Dick, really, and very obliging. Be nice to him, do!"

"I'm always nice to him—I'm always nice to everyone," said Dick, with his candid self-approval. And what he said was true. Niceness came naturally to all the Kendalls.

From his appearance Mr. Murgatroyd might have been a generation older than Neil Kendall instead of actually, by a narrow margin, the younger man. It was he who had arranged for them to rent the despised bungalow, and at very short notice too—a cable sent from New York: "Sailing *Queen Elizabeth* tomorrow stop please organize two month furnished lease Home Counties stop eternally grateful bless you Molly." And it was he also who had produced the Old Rectory for them nearly a decade earlier when they had taken the momentous decision to settle down in the country *permanently*. Over the years William Murgatroyd had often come in useful to the Kendalls. They paid for his many services—and in their view, considering he was such a colossal bore, paid handsomely—by being nice to him.

Mr. Murgatroyd said that it was a business call he was making on behalf of the owner of the bungalow who was in Scotland, and who had apparently received no response from his tenant to any of the numerous letters he had sent him. "You must reply," said Mr. Murgatroyd severely. Neil Kendall was lazily reassuring: so he would, in a week or two, when their plans had been finalized. But his friend the entomologist, with a mixture of diffidence and obstinacy, insisted on the landlord being written to that same afternoon. "You can't keep him hanging about at the end of a string to suit yourself, Neil—it's a thorough nuisance for him. He has to make plans too."

"Oh, very well," said Neil Kendall, sounding sulky. And he went huffily into the bungalow, slamming the door. The younger Kendalls pulled naughty faces behind their visitor's back. Mrs. Kendall held on to his hand entreatingly and besought him to stay for tea.

"Do stop fussing, William darling, and sit down and be sociable—"

Mr. Murgatroyed refused to stay for tea. Elsie found herself walking up the path beside him, pushing her bike. She had neither properly said goodbye, nor yet—so as to give it any real significance—not said goodbye. Her leave-taking had been of no more consequence to the Kendalls than the leave-taking of old Muggins, in whose company they had so lightheartedly, with smiling half-averted faces, waved her off. She groaned in spirit: how stupid of her to have imagined she had anything to offer them—she had nothing! There were scores of sixteen-year-old girls in Paris, in America, as pretty—*far prettier!*—than she was. Elsie longed to jump on her bicycle and pedal away out of Croxham as fast as she could, away, away, and never come back. But good manners forbade such abrupt behavior and instead she dawdled along, mutely agonized, at the side of the Kendalls' dull old friend.

William Murgatroyd knew she was bleeding; he had

bled too, in his time. Being a compassionate man, as well as an expert on beetles, he was very sorry for her. What could he say, though, in a few sentences as they ambled down the village street together, that would stanch those wounds? His experience of the Kendalls was a long one. He had been at university with Neil Kendall. Unlike Neil, he had arrived at university from grammar school. There was indeed, education excepted, a similarity between his background and Elsie's. He too had been the solitary child of affectionate parents; his Bingley, a small provincial town in the north of England where his father kept a chemist instead of a sweet shop.

Elsie was unaware of it, but Mr. Murgatroyd had often seen her before, playing with Louisa at Bingley Old Rectory. He had been struck then, he remembered, by some quality in the little girl deeper than mere quietness: a patient watchful expectancy. And he remembered also what Molly Kendall had said of Louisa's companion: "Goodness knows how Neil and I would stand the strain of being boxed up here in term time with Louisa not at boarding school if it weren't for that child from the sweet shop. She's a perfect godsend—and so handy, living just down the road."

The child from the sweet shop was older now. Mr. Murgatroyd said to her: "You have my admiration, let me tell you, for dropping in on that family unannounced. I couldn't have done it at your age, not if I'd been paid in gold."

Roused from her trance of misery, Elsie glanced up at him, startled. Was he rebuking her? mocking her? His eyes were not blue and dazzling, as the Kendalls' eyes were, but they were peculiarly bright behind their spectacles, and penetrating: she saw that when they looked at her they really saw her, as the Kendalls' blue eyes never did. "It was

an act of courage," said Mr. Murgatroyd. He raised his
Panama hat an inch in a gesture of homage to all acts of
courage, hers included. They had stopped in front of a
neat gray stone house fronting the pavement. "This is
where I live. Would you care to come in and have a cup of
tea with me?"

"Oh, no—no, thank you." She shook her head. "I must
get on home to Bingley." The word "goodbye" was too
difficult for her lips to frame. Grateful to him, she hesi-
tated. "I suppose you couldn't do with a couple of lettuces,
could you?" She undid the straps of her saddlebag. "Oh
dear, what a pity—I'm afraid it's too late. It's been such a
hot day—they're dead."

All at once the tears began to gush down her cheeks. Mr.
Murgatroyd had no experience of young girls, and certainly not of young girls who wept openly in the street.
Shyness prevented him from lending her his handkerchief.
"Perhaps," he said as an alternative, "you would come and
have tea with me next week? Next Sunday, at four—would
that be convenient? They don't mean to be unkind," he
added, moved by the extremity of her grief to try to sal-
vage something for her comfort. "They don't know that
they are. They don't know what it's like, Elsie, to be you—
or me; only what it's like to be a Kendall."

Elsie, lacking a handkerchief, put out her tongue and
licked off as many tears as she could reach with it. Exhausted and speechless, hiccuping, sniffing, she yet managed as she clambered on her bike to nod at Mr. Murgatroyd. The nod meant, as she trusted he would understand:
"I'll see you next Sunday, then."

# The Real Thing

## WILLIAM TREVOR

He had, romantically, a bad reputation. He had a wife and several children. His carry-on with Sarah Spence was a legend among a generation of girls, and the story was that none of it had stopped with Sarah Spence. His old red Ford Escort had been reported drawn up in quiet lay-bys; often he spent weekends away from home; Annie Green had come across him going somewhere on a train once, alone and morose in the buffet car. Nobody's parents were aware of the facts about him, nor were the other staff, nor even the boys at the school. His carry-on with Sarah Spence, and coming across him or his car, were a little tapestry of secrets that suddenly was yours when you became fifteen and a senior, a member of 2A. For the rest of your time at Foxfield Comprehensive—for the rest of your life, preferably—you didn't breathe a word to people whose business it wasn't.

It was understandable when you looked at him that parents and staff didn't guess. It was also understandable that his activities were protected by the senior girls. He was forty years old. He had dark hair with a little gray in it, and a face that was boyish—like a French boy's, someone had once said, and the description had stuck, often to be repeated. There was a kind of ragamuffin innocence about his eyes. The cast of his lips suggested a melancholy nature and his smile, when it came, had sadness in it too. His name was Mr. Tennyson. His subject was English.

Jenny, arriving one September in 2A, learned all about him. She remembered Sarah Spence, a girl at the top of the school when she had been at the bottom, tall and beautiful. He carried on because he was unhappily married, she was informed. Consider where he lived even: trapped in a tiny gate lodge on the Ilminster road because he couldn't afford anything better, trapped with a wife and children when he deserved freedom. Would he one day publish poetry as profound as his famous namesake's, though of course more up-to-date? Or was his talent lost forever? One way or the other he was made for love.

It seemed to Jenny that the girls of 2A eyed one another, wondering which among them would become a successor to Sarah Spence. They eyed the older girls, of Class 1, 1A, and 1B, wondering which of them was already her successor, discreetly taking her place in the red Ford Escort on dusky afternoons. He would never be coarse, you couldn't imagine coarseness in him. He'd never try anything unpleasant, he'd never in a million years fumble at you. He'd just be there, being himself, smelling faintly of fresh tobacco, the fingers of a hand perhaps brushing your arm by accident.

"Within the play," he suggested in his soft voice, almost a whisper, "order is represented by the royal house of Scotland. We must try and remember Shakespeare's point of view, how Shakespeare saw these things."

They were studying *Macbeth* and *Huckleberry Finn* with him, but when he talked about Shakespeare it seemed more natural and suited to him than when he talked about Mark Twain.

"On Duncan's death," he said, "should the natural order continue, his son Malcolm would become king. Already Duncan has indicated—by making Malcolm Prince of Cumberland—that he considers him capable of ruling."

Jenny had pale fair hair, the color of ripened wheat. It fell from a divide at the center of her head, two straight lines on either side of a thin face. Her eyes were large and of a faded blue. She was lanky, with legs which she considered to be too long but which her mother said she'd be thankful for one day.

"Disruption is everywhere, remember," he said. "Disruption in nature as well as in the royal house. Shakespeare insinuates a comparison between what is happening in human terms and in terms of nature. On the night of Duncan's death there is a sudden storm in which chimneys are blown off and houses shaken. Mysterious screams are heard. Horses go wild. A falcon is killed by a mousing owl."

Listening to him, it seemed to Jenny that she could listen forever, no matter what he said. At night, lying in bed with her eyes closed, she delighted in leisurely fantasies, of having breakfast with him and ironing his clothes, of walking beside him on a seashore or sitting beside him in his old Ford Escort. There was a particular story she repeated to herself: that she was on the promenade at Lyme Regis and that he came up to her and asked her if she'd like to go for a walk. They walked up to the cliffs and then along the cliff path, and everything was different from Foxfield Comprehensive because a play he'd written was going to be done on the radio and another one on the London stage. "Oh, darling," she said, daring to say it. "Oh, Jenny," he said.

Terms and holidays went by. Once, just before the Easter of that year, she met him with his wife, shopping in the International Stores in Ilminster. They had two of their four children with them, little boys with freckles. His wife had freckles also. She was a woman like a sack of something, Jenny considered, with thick, unhealthy-looking legs. He was pushing a trolley full of breakfast cereals and wrapped bread, and tins. Even though he didn't speak to her or even appear to see her, it was a stroke of luck to come across him in the town because he didn't often come into the village. Foxfield had only half a dozen shops and the Bow and Arrow public house even though it was enormous, a sprawling dormitory village that had had the new Comprehensive added to all the other new building in 1969. Because of the position of the Tennysons' gate lodge it was clearly more convenient for them to shop in Ilminster.

"Hullo, Mr. Tennyson," she said in the International Stores, and he turned and looked at her. He nodded and smiled.

Jenny moved into 1A at the end of that school year. She wondered if he'd noticed how her breasts had become bigger during the time she'd been in 2A, and how her complexion had definitely improved. Her breasts were quite presentable now, which was a relief because she'd had a fear that they weren't going to develop at all. She wondered if he'd noticed her Green Magic eye shadow. Everyone said it suited her, except her father, who always blew up over things like that. Once she heard one of the new kids saying she was the prettiest girl in the school. Adam Swann and Chinny Martin from 1B kept hanging about, trying to chat her up. Chinny Martin even wrote her notes.

"You're mooning," her father said. "You don't take a pick of notice these days."

"Exams," her mother hastily interjected and afterwards, when Jenny was out of the room, quite sharply reminded her husband that adolescence was a difficult time for girls. It was best not to remark on things.

"I didn't mean a criticism, Ellie," Jenny's father protested, aggrieved.

"They take it as a criticism. Every word. They're edgy, see."

He sighed. He was a painter and decorator, with his own business. Jenny was their only child. There'd been four miscarriages, all of which might have been boys, which naturally were what he'd wanted, with the business. He'd have to sell it one day, but it didn't matter all that much when you thought about it. Having miscarriages was worse than selling a business, more depressing really. A woman's lot was harder than a man's, he'd decided long ago.

"Broody," his wife diagnosed. "Just normal broody. She'll see her way through it."

Every evening her parents sat in their clean, neat sitting room watching television. Her mother made tea at nine o'clock because it was nice to have a cup with the News. She always called upstairs to Jenny, but Jenny never wanted to have tea or see the News. She did her homework in her bedroom, a small room that was clean and neat also, with a pebbly cream wallpaper expertly hung by her father. At half past ten she usually went down to the kitchen and made herself some Ovaltine. She drank it at the table, with the cat, Tinkle, on her lap. Her mother usually came in with the tea things to wash up, and they might chat, the conversation consisting mainly of gossip from Foxfield Comprehensive, although never of course containing a reference to Mr. Tennyson. Sometimes Jenny didn't feel like chatting and wouldn't, feigning sleepiness. If she sat there long enough her father would come in to fetch himself a cup of water because he always liked to have one near him in the night. He couldn't help glancing at her eye shadow when he said good night and she could see him making an effort not to mention it, having doubtless been told not to by her mother. They did their best. She liked them very much. She loved them, she supposed.

But not in the way she loved Mr. Tennyson. "Robert Tennyson," she murmured to herself in bed. "Oh, Robert dear." Softly his lips were there, and the smell of fresh tobacco made her swoon, forcing her to close her eyes. "Oh, yes," she said. "Oh, yes, yes." He lifted the dress over her head. His hands were taut, charged with their shared passion. "My love," he said in his soft voice, almost a whisper. Every night before she went to sleep his was the face that entirely filled her mind. Had it once not been there she would have thought herself faithless. And every morning, in a ceremonial way, she conjured it up again, first thing, pride of place.

Coming out of Harper's the news agents' one Saturday afternoon, she found waiting for her, not Mr. Tennyson, but Chinny Martin, with his motorcycle on its pedestal in the street. He asked her if she'd like to go for a spin into the country and offered to supply her with a crash helmet. He was wearing a crash helmet himself, a bulbous red object with a peak and a windshield that fitted over his eyes. He was also wearing heavy plastic gloves, red also, and a red windcheater. He was smiling at her, the spots on his pronounced chin more noticeable after exposure to the weather on his motorcycle. His eyes were serious, closely fixed on hers.

She shook her head at him. There was hardly anything she'd have disliked more than a ride into the country with Chinny Martin, her arms half round his waist, a borrowed crash helmet making her feel silly. He'd stop the motorcycle in a suitable place and he'd suggest something like a walk to the river or to some old ruin or into a wood. He'd suggest sitting down here and then he'd begin to fumble at her, and his chin would be sticking into her face, cold and unpleasant. His fingernails would be engrained, as the fingernails of boys who owned motorcycles always were.

"Thanks all the same," she said.

"Come on, Jenny."

"No, I'm busy. Honestly. I'm working at home."

It couldn't have been pleasant, being called Chinny just because you had a jutting chin. Nicknames were horrible: there was a boy called Nut Adams and another called Wet Small and a girl called Kisses. Chinny Martin's name was Clive, but she'd never heard anyone calling him that. She felt sorry for him, standing there in his crash helmet and his special clothes. He'd probably planned it all, working it out that she'd be impressed by his gear and his motorcycle. But of course she wasn't. *Yamaha* it said on the petrol tank of the motorcycle, and there was a girl in a swimsuit which he had presumably stuck onto the tank himself. The girl's swimsuit was yellow and so was her hair, which was streaming out behind her, as if caught in a wind. The petrol tank was black.

"Jenny," he said, lowering his voice so that it became almost croaky. "Listen, Jenny—"

"Sorry."

She began to walk away, up the village street, but he walked beside her, pushing the Yamaha.

"I love you, Jenny," he said.

She laughed because she felt embarrassed.

"I can't bear not seeing you, Jenny."

"Oh, well—"

"Jenny."

They were passing the petrol pumps, the Orchard Garage. Mr. Batten was on the pavement, wiping oil from his hands with a rag. "How's he running?" he called out to Chinny Martin, referring to the Yamaha, but Chinny Martin ignored the question.

"I think of you all the time, Jenny."

"Oh, Clive, don't be silly." She felt silly herself, calling him by his proper name.

"D'you like me, Jenny?"

"Of course I like you." She smiled at him, trying to cover up the lie: she didn't particularly like him, she didn't particularly not. She just felt sorry for him, with his noticeable chin and the nickname it had given him. His father worked in the powdered milk factory. He'd do the same: you could guess that all too easily.

"Come for a ride with me, Jenny."

"No, honestly."

"Why not then?"

"It's better not to start anything, Clive. Look, don't write me notes."

"Don't you like my notes?"

"I don't want to start anything."

"There's someone else is there, Jenny? Adam Swann? Rick Hayes?"

He sounded like a character in a television serial; he sounded sloppy and stupid.

"If you knew how I feel about you," he said, lowering his voice even more. "I love you like anything. It's the real thing."

"I like you too, Clive. Only not in that way," she hastily added.

"Wouldn't you ever? Wouldn't you even try?"

"I've told you."

"Rick Hayes's only after sex."

"I don't like Rick Hayes."

"Any girl with legs on her is all he wants."

"Yes, I know."

"I can't concentrate on things, Jenny. I think of you the entire time."

"I'm sorry."

"Oh God, Jenny."

She turned into the Mace shop just to escape. She picked up a wire basket and pretended to be looking at tins of cat food. She heard the roar of the Yamaha as her admirer rode away, and it seemed all wrong that he should have gone like that, so noisily when he was so upset.

At home she thought about the incident. It didn't in the least displease her that a boy had passionately proclaimed love for her. It even made her feel quite elated. She felt pleasantly warm when she thought about it, and the feeling bewildered her. That she, so much in love with someone else, should be moved in the very least by the immature protestations of a youth from 1B was a mystery. She even considered telling her mother about the incident, but in the end decided not to. "Quite sprightly, she seems," she heard her father murmuring.

"In every line of that sonnet," Mr. Tennyson said the following Monday afternoon, "there is evidence of the richness that makes Shakespeare not just our own greatest writer but the world's as well."

She listened, enthralled, physically pleasured by the utterance of each syllable. There was a tiredness about his boyish eyes, as if he hadn't slept. His wife had probably been bothering him, wanting him to do jobs around the house when he should have been writing sonnets of his own. She imagined him unable to sleep, lying there worrying about things, about his life. She imagined his wife like a grampus beside him, her mouth open, her upper lip as coarse as a man's.

"When forty winters shall besiege thy brow," he said, "And dig deep trenches in thy beauty's field."

*Dear Jenny*, a note that morning from Chinny Martin had said. *I just want to be with you. I just want to talk to you. Please come out with me.*

"Jenny, stay a minute," Mr. Tennyson said when the bell went. "Your essay."

Immediately there was tension among the girls of 1A, as if the English master had caused threads all over the classroom to become taut. Unaware, the boys proceeded as they always did, throwing books into their briefcases and sauntering into the corridor. The girls lingered over anything they could think of. Jenny approached Mr. Tennyson's desk.

"It's very good," he said, opening her essay book. "But you're getting too fond of using three little dots at the end of a sentence. The sentence should imply the dots. It's like underlining to suggest emphasis, a bad habit also."

One by one the girls dribbled from the classroom, leaving behind them the shreds of their reluctance. Out of all of them he had chosen her: was she to be another Sarah Spence, or just some kind of stopgap, like other girls since Sarah Spence were rumored to have been? But as he continued to talk about her essay—called "Belief in Ghosts"—she wondered if she'd even be a stopgap. His fingers didn't once brush the back of her hand. His French boy's eyes didn't linger once on hers.

"I've kept you late," he said in the end.

"That's all right, sir."

"You will try to keep your sentences short? Your descriptions have a way of becoming too complicated."

"I'll try, sir."

"I really enjoyed that essay."

He handed her the exercise book and then, without any doubt whatsoever, he smiled meaningfully into her eyes. She felt herself going hot. Her hands became clammy. She just stood there while his glance passed over her eye shadow, over her nose and cheeks, over her mouth.

"You're very pretty," he said.

"Thank you, sir."

Her voice reminded her of the croak in Chinny Martin's when he'd been telling her he loved her. She tried to smile, but could not. She wanted his hand to reach out and push her gently away from him so that he could see her properly. But it didn't. He stared into her eyes again, as if endeavoring to ascertain their precise shade of blue.

"You look like a girl we had here once," he said. "Called Sarah Spence."

"I remember Sarah Spence."

"She was good at English too."

She wanted something to happen, thunder to begin, or a torrent of rain, anything that would keep them in the classroom. She couldn't even bear the thought of walking to her desk and putting her essay book in her briefcase.

"Sarah went to Warwick University," he said.

She nodded. She tried to smile again and this time the smile came. She said to herself that it was a brazen smile and she didn't care. She hoped it made her seem more than ever like Sarah Spence, sophisticated and able for anything. She wondered if he said to all the girls who were stopgaps that they looked like Sarah Spence. She didn't care. His carry-on with Sarah Spence was over and done with, he didn't even see her anymore. By all accounts Sarah Spence had let him down, but never in a million years would she. She would wait for him forever, or until the divorce came through. When he was old she would look after him.

"You better be getting home, Jenny."

"I don't want to, sir."

She continued to stand there, the exercise book in her left hand. She watched while some kind of shadow passed over his face. For a moment his eyes closed.

"Why don't you want to go?" he said.

"Because I'm in love with you, sir."

"You mustn't be, Jenny."

"Why not?"

"You know why not."

"What about Sarah Spence?"

"Sarah was different."

"I don't care how many stopgaps you've had. I don't care. I don't love you any less."

"Stopgaps, Jenny?"

"The ones you made do with."

"Made do?" He was suddenly frowning at her, his face screwed up a little. "Made do?" he said again.

"The other girls. The ones who reminded you of her."

"There weren't any other girls."

"You were seen, sir—"

"Only Sarah and I were seen."

"Your car—"

"Give a dog a bad name, Jenny. There weren't any others."

She felt iciness inside her, somewhere in her stomach. Other girls had formed an attachment for him, as she had. Other girls had probably stood on this very spot, telling him. It was that, and the reality of Sarah Spence, that had turned him into a schoolgirls' legend. Only Sarah Spence had gone with him in his old Ford Escort to quiet lay-bys, only Sarah Spence had felt his arms around her. Why shouldn't he be seen in the buffet car of a train, alone? The weekends he'd spent away from home were probably with a sick mother.

"I'm no Casanova, Jenny."

"I had to tell you I'm in love with you, sir. I couldn't not."

"It's no good loving me, I'm afraid."

"You're the nicest person I'll ever know."

"No, I'm not, Jenny. I'm just an English teacher who took advantage of a young girl's infatuation. Shabby, people would say."

"You're not shabby. Oh God, you're not shabby." She heard her own voice crying out shrilly, close to tears. It astonished her. It was unbelievable that she should be so violently protesting. It was unbelievable that he should have called himself shabby.

"She had an abortion in Warwick," he said, "after a weekend we spent in a hotel. I let that happen, Jenny."

"You couldn't help it."

"Of course I could have helped it."

Without wanting to, she imagined them in the hotel he spoke of. She imagined them having a meal, sitting opposite each other at a table, and a waiter placing plates in front of them. She imagined them in their bedroom, a grimy room with a lace curtain drawn across the lower part of the single window and a washbasin in a corner. The bedroom had featured in a film she'd seen, and Sarah Spence was even like the actress who had played the part of a shopgirl. She stood there in her underclothes just as the shopgirl had, awkwardly waiting while he smiled his love at her. "Then let not winter's ragged hand deface," he whispered, "In thee thy summer, ere thou be distilled. Oh Sarah, love." He took the underclothes from her body, as the actor in the film had, all the time whispering sonnets.

"It was messy and horrible," he said. "That's how it ended, Jenny."

"I don't care how it ended. I'd go with you anywhere. I'd go to a thousand hotels."

"No, no, Jenny."

"I love you terribly."

She wept, still standing there. He got down from the stool in front of his desk and came and put his arms about her, telling her to cry. He said that tears were good, not bad. He made her sit down at a desk and then he sat down beside her. His love affair with Sarah Spence sounded romantic, he said, and because of its romantic sheen girls fell in love with him. They fell in love with the unhappiness they sensed in him. He found it hard to stop them.

"I should move away from here," he said, "but I can't bring myself to do it. Because she'll always come back to see her family and whenever she does I can catch a glimpse of her."

It was the same as she felt about him, like the glimpse that day in the International Stores. It was the same as Chinny Martin hanging about outside Harper's. And yet of course it wasn't the same as Chinny Martin. How could it possibly be? Chinny Martin was stupid and unprepossessing and ordinary.

"I'd be better to you," she cried out in sudden desperation, unable to prevent herself. Clumsily she put a hand on his shoulder, and clumsily took it away again. "I would wait forever," she said, sobbing, knowing she looked ugly.

He waited for her to calm down. He stood up and after a moment so did she. She walked with him from the classroom, down the corridor and out of the door that led to the car park.

"You can't just leave," he said, "a wife and four children. It was hard to explain that to Sarah. She hates me now."

He unlocked the driver's door of the Ford Escort. He smiled at her. He said:

"There's no one else I can talk to about her. Except girls like you. You mustn't feel embarrassed in class, Jenny."

He drove away, not offering her a lift, which he might have done, for their direction was the same. She didn't in the least look like Sarah Spence: he'd probably said the same thing to all the others, the infatuated girls he could talk to about the girl he loved. The little scenes in the classroom, the tears, the talk: all that brought him closer to Sarah Spence. The love of a girl he didn't care about warmed him, as Chinny Martin's love had warmed her too, even though Chinny Martin was ridiculous.

She walked across the car park, imagining him driving back to his gate lodge with Sarah Spence alive again in his mind, loving her more than ever. "Jenny," the voice of Chinny Martin called out, coming from nowhere.

He was there, standing by his Yamaha, beside a car. She shook her head at him, and began to run. At home she would sit and eat in the kitchen with her parents, who wouldn't be any different. She would escape and lie on her bed in her small neat bedroom, longing to be where she'd never be now, beside him in his car, or on a train, or anywhere. "Jenny," the voice of Chinny Martin called out again, silly with his silly love.

# The Return

## PEGGY WOODFORD

I often think about love. I sit on my window seat gazing
out at the bare trees on the Common, and think about love,
and Joël and me, and what on earth the future can possibly
hold for me because I have already met my love, my real,
true, only love. He is dead; and I am still eighteen. I can't
believe a love as deep and total as ours can come to any
human twice. Perfect things are unique, after all.

Before we met, Joël and I were two ordinary teenagers,
but after we fell in love our lives grew magic dimensions.
We thought alike, and felt alike, and found each other
beautiful. We could stare into each other's eyes for hours,
literally hours; our gaze was like a conversation, and just
now and then we'd touch each other's cheek or ear or chin
and smile. We were so together we were almost beyond
happiness. And then Joël died suddenly, snap, just like
that, and I was left with two of my four walls gone.

"Mary! *Mary*. Telephone."

"Who is it?"

"Paul."

Not again. I heaved myself off the window seat and
went half-unwillingly downstairs. I shivered; the telephone
was in a drafty part of the hall and my room had been

snug. Paul wanted me to go round to his place that evening and listen to records but I refused. I liked Paul well enough; I liked several boys I knew; but how could they begin to match up to Joël? I always told them about Joël and it usually put them off. But nothing seemed to put Paul off.

"Why can't you come?"

"None of your business."

"You just can't be bothered, can you?"

"It's not that, Paul—"

"Oh, go on."

"All right. I can't be bothered. You said it first."

"God, you're hopeless."

He rang off, and I promptly wished I had said I'd go. But by the time I had reached my room again I was glad I'd stayed. My room is my fortress; I love it for all sorts of reasons, but mainly because it is where Joël is most alive. I have thought about him there for so many hours that sometimes (though not recently) his independent presence seems to have been in the room.

Near my bed is a shelf where I keep my most precious things, the three most precious of all being the photographs I possess of Joël. Only three; not very much to remember his face by. One is of him here in our garden; my father took it, a group photograph in which everyone looks a bit sheepish. I remember my father saying: "Come on, everyone, out on the lawn, I've got one exposure left and I want to develop the film." And so by good luck I have one photograph of Joël and me together.

The second photograph is a small, dog-eared one Joël once sent me, taken of him on the beach in Brittany by a friend. He is kneeling in the sand, grinning. I love it. He was sixteen then.

And the last photograph shows him solemn and stiff; his

parents sent it to me several months after his death. They had had it blown up from some snapshot, and to my mind had chosen a picture which caught none of his real self. He looked handsome, but as I said, solemn and stiff. My gay, vivid Joël. It was the sort of photograph the French choose to put into everlasting frames on their tombstones. I have never been back to see Joël's grave; I do not know what sort of tombstone the Jouberts chose; perhaps they had even used that photograph. I did not know and I didn't want to know. That part of Brittany has crumbled off my life's map. Joël is dead. The places I loved him in are dead too.

Late that evening as I was going down to the bathroom I overheard my parents talking about me. Without quite meaning to, I froze.

"—and so *rude* to everyone. I really am beginning to give up."

"I agree she's in a particularly tedious state." I could hear my father walking round the bedroom. "But she's working hard, and in general copes well enough."

"Too well. She's too controlled. All these boys come after her, and she's cold, uninterested. Just goes upstairs and gazes at her bloody photographs."

"My love, don't get too angry. It was bound to affect her profoundly and for a long time. It's only eighteen months since the boy died."

"But she's not getting any *better*. You know what I mean. I feel as if she's deliberately trying to keep the whole thing alive in her mind. It just isn't healthy at all. She's made a sort of *shrine* to Joël in her room."

I wanted to creep away, but was afraid of making a noise. I heard drawers open and shut, and my father saying:

"I don't seem to have any clean vests left."

"Sorry, love. I've got a bit behind schedule, it's been such a hectic week at work. There might be a clean one in the airing cupboard. I'll have a look."

"Tomorrow will do."

But my mother was already out on the landing. There I was, caught in the act, with no hope of escape. My mother looked at me, and I looked at my mother. Nobody said anything for an aeon of time. Then my mother tossed her head in a special way she had.

"Did you hear all that?"

"Yes."

"Well, I'm glad. *Glad*."

My father, in underpants, appeared at the bedroom door. "Steady, Ginny." He hated rows, and he stared at us both in despair.

"I think you're exaggerating."

"Exaggerating? You *must* be joking. Anyway, exaggerations apart, I'm glad you've heard the truth at last."

"The truth? All I heard was your opinions." I stuck my hands in my jeans pockets.

"Now, Mary—"

"Oh, let her talk, Robin. She's lived behind plate glass for too long."

"I haven't made an altar to Joël."

"You have, Mary. You have. You must put his death behind you, not try to keep it fresh in your mind all the time."

"It is fresh in my mind."

"I don't believe you. You deliberately keep it fresh because you're afraid of it dying, of forgetting him."

"That's not true—how could I forget him—" I kept my hands in my pockets, but I was shaking all over.

"You *will* forget him. Life's like that." She tried to make her voice gentle, but I could hear the sharp impatience behind it.

"You don't understand. You don't understand. No one you have really loved has died. You just don't understand."

My father barked: "Go to bed. Just go to bed, will you." My mother gazed at me emptily. I ran upstairs, and lay down, too angry even to cry. Stiff, rigid, I lay. Then I rolled over and looked at my photographs. An altar. How dare she. I picked up the three photographs of my love, my love, my love. I put them in a drawer. All right, Georgina Meredith, I will have my altar out of sight.

The door opened and I jumped. I shut the drawer quietly. My father, now in his dressing gown, came in and sat down.

"Mary."

I paced about.

"Cool down."

"I am cool."

He snorted. Then he yawned, and because his yawns were especially catching, so did I. We grinned at each other feebly.

"You're a bad girl, eavesdropping like that."

"I didn't mean to; I was on my way to the loo." I saw my father's eyes focus on the bare shelf, but he said nothing. "Anyway, if that's how Mum feels I'm glad I know it."

"You have no idea what she feels. You made that quite plain by your insensitive remarks."

My father's voice was icy. I swallowed.

"She knows precisely what it's like to lose someone beloved. You seem to have forgotten that her favorite brother was killed in the war. You seem to have also forgotten that her father died only two years ago."

I wanted to say it was not the same, but no words would come.

"It is arrogant and conceited of you to think you have a monopoly on grief. Joël's sudden death was very very sad, but death is death, the same for old king and young beggarmaid. Those left behind grieve with the same emotions."

"But some grieve longer than others because they've lost more."

"Granted."

"That was my point."

"It was also your mother's point. She expected you to feel it deeply and for a long time. You have. But she now feels you've become a professional griever. You're mourning for the sake of it."

"Thanks. Thanks very much."

"You are, Mary. Whether you like it or not, you are." He got up and came and put an arm round my shoulders. I stood like a ramrod. "No one is going to start thinking that your love for Joël is suspect just because you stop thinking about him and no longer keep his memory in the center of your life."

I wanted him to stop talking and go away. I hated him prying into my feelings. I stood rigid, said nothing. He looked at my face in silence for a moment, kissed me good night and left. I went to the window, dragged back the curtain, and stared out into the darkness. I wanted to go outside and run and run through the cold air until I was exhausted. I sat down on my bed to put my shoes on again, and then found my energy draining away into depression and misery.

Eventually I undressed and got into bed, leaving my clothes in a heap on the floor. I switched off the light and lay staring blankly into the darkness. Something I had forgotten niggled at my brain. Then, cold, I realized what it was: I always put my favorite photograph of Joël under my pillow, and tonight I had forgotten. I got up and fetched it, kissed it and put it under my head. Joël, Joël. I lay thinking about him as I always did. He was a very long way away; the shadows in my mind were thin now. I fought each day to keep my memories vivid; why, oh why were they fading. I hadn't changed. Oh, Joël. Joël. In the end tears did come, but even as they came I knew that they were for my useless memory failing him, and not for him, not for him.

Despite the fact I gave him little encouragement, Paul kept coming to see me. One day he arrived with tickets for a concert in a local church.

"Will you come?"

"I don't know much about music."

"Nor do I. That doesn't stop us going."

The church wasn't very full, and Paul led me right to the front pew, where there was still room.

"Let's sit where we can really see."

I was wearing my scruffiest jeans and a very old jersey; I felt slightly self-conscious until we settled down in our seats. Paul looked eagerly about him, interested in the church. I find all churches depressing; they are so *mute* yet well cared for, so polished and scrubbed. It's so suburban. This church was no exception; it was full of clean smells and shining brass.

Paul's family are Jewish; he told me his grandparents are still orthodox, but his parents had both given up the practice of their religion when young. I looked sideways at Paul; he didn't look in the least "Jewish"; he was fair with light-colored eyes. His eyebrows and eyelashes were dark.

He suddenly looked round and met my gaze. For a moment our eyes stayed linked.

Then we both started to talk busily about books we had read. Paul talked about a book as if he was discussing a friend; he didn't use any critical jargon. I was beginning to have the nasty feeling that he was better educated than I was. As I had long ago decided that culture is the only thing left worth living for, it was a bit galling to find someone who approached it all so lightly to be equally well read. And he also, it turned out, knew quite a lot about music; I discovered he played the cello.

"I thought you said you didn't know much about music."

"I don't. I'm a lousy cellist. I only keep it up because it would be silly to drop it."

During the interval we wandered about outside the church. I did not know quite how or when it had happened, but there was a difference in our relationship. Instead of just suffering his presence, I was enjoying myself. Whether he was as well I don't know, but he stopped being hesitant and apologetic, and was witty and amusing. It occurred to me that until now I hadn't known the real Paul at all.

We went back into the church. The work in the second half was Schubert's String Quintet in C major; I knew it a little, but had never listened to it properly, and never in performance. It ravished me, it absolutely ravished me. And as it finished an idea came into my head. It came from nowhere, fully grown. Unexpected though it was, I knew I would have to carry it out. I put it to simmer at the back of my mind.

"Thank you for taking me. That was good."

Paul stood on the pavement outside our house, yawning.

"Though they didn't play it very well, it was worth hearing."

"I thought they played beautifully."

"The viola was weak."

"Well it all sounded fine to me." He was spoiling my evening, and I felt angry. I waited for him to suggest, as he usually did, our next meeting.

"Good night," he said, and with a wave walked off.


"Was it good?"

"Lovely."

"You sounded bowled over." My father was carrying a tray downstairs.

"I'm tired, that's all. You expect everyone to be wildly cheerful all the time."

"Ginny has retired to bed feeling ill. Go and see her, I'm sure she'd like to hear about the concert." He went on downstairs.

My mother looked rotten, exhausted and ill. She had a tattered old shawl round her shoulders, and with her drawn face and shut eyes, it made her look old. I stood still; I could see what she'd look like at seventy. She opened her eyes.

"Hullo, Mum. Dad said you'd retired to bed. How do you feel?"

"Shaky." She patted the bed and I sat down. We chatted for a while. I found I wanted to tell her about my new idea.

"Mum, I've got a plan. You might think it's mad, but I want to go to France this Whitsun; we've got a week off at half term."

"Tell me more. Why France?"

It was hard to say. "I think I want to go and see Joël's grave." I heard my father's footsteps on the stairs. I put my

finger to my lips and whispered: "Don't tell anyone about
it." I did not want my father's sardonic comments. My
mother stared at me looking puzzled. She pulled her shawl
closer round her shoulders and thanked my father for the
glass of whatever it was he put beside her. He spilled a little
and they fussed about mopping it up with tissues.

"Good night," I said. They answered me absent-mindedly, being concerned about marks on the antique bedside
table. Why they bother with antiques when they are such
a constant worry, I don't know. I'm for utility myself.

When I got to my own room I found I couldn't settle
down to a good read. I felt uneasy and tense for some
reason; perhaps it was this new idea about France which
was unsettling me. I went to have a bath, and lay trying to
plan my trip. It was hard to work out. If I hitchhiked I'd
have to go with someone, and even then I wasn't sure my
parents would let me. I could not afford to go by train or
plane. The whole idea now depressed me, and yet I knew
that somehow I would have to carry it out. I went to bed
worrying about it, and it was only in the morning that I
realized, as I felt my pillow, that I had not put Joël's photograph there. I had completely forgotten for the first
time. I felt so guilty I did not even open the drawer where
the photographs lay.

That evening I shut myself up and got out all my letters
from Joël, which were tied up in a bundle with mine to
him. I read them again, and looked at the face that had
written them. I even put on my old well-worn Jacques
Brel record of the song "Ne me quitte pas" which he and
I had loved so much, and I loved still. But I knew as I did
all these things that it was pointless, Joël was going. Ne
me quitte pas, ne me quitte pas. I could not bear it.

Paul took me to a marvelous party. I even wore a party
dress; my mother, hearing me say I'd go if I could wear my

jeans, I never wore anything else, came back from work with a beautiful Indian cotton caftan which was so unexpected I found myself trying it on. I liked wearing it. It was loose and easy and didn't ask me to live up to it. Paul obviously liked it too.

The party was a small one, given by some friends of his I didn't know very well. We all laughed and danced a lot. I haven't enjoyed myself so much for ages. Paul walked me home by midnight but I knew he was going back to the party and staying there for the night.

"How super the Muirs are."

"Aren't they."

"You have such nice friends."

Paul didn't answer. We negotiated a large intersection with several roads crossing. I suddenly found myself saying: "I've got to go to France at Whitsun. Will you come with me?"

Paul stared down at the pavement. I sensed his horror.

"It's a trip I've got to make and my parents won't let me go on my own. There's a place I've got to see." I was babbling, and it sounded lame, ridiculous. Paul looked puzzled and unenthusiastic, even hunted. By now we were at our house and I said quickly: "Don't worry, forget it. I'm not really serious, I don't suppose I'll go in the end. Thanks for a fantastic evening." I went quickly into the house, unable to keep my smile going any longer. Once inside I sat down on the bottom step of the staircase and groaned. I was *stupid* to have asked him; why on earth had I done it, particularly as I had planned to ask Jilly. I had spoiled everything, scared him off forever. I ground my teeth.

"Is that you, Mary?" My mother's whisper.

"No, just a big hairy burglar having a rest on the stairs."

"Was it fun?"

"Smashing. The best party I've ever been to."

"I *am* glad. Was your dress a success?"

"Lots of people said they liked it."

"Good. I suppose Paul brought you back—"

"Yes, he did." I kissed her good night and hurried to bed. She liked post-mortems, I didn't.

Paul kept away, as I feared he would. I went over my stupidity again and again in my mind, wondering how to put things right as lightly as possible. But you can't put someone's mind at ease without seeing them or talking to them, or even writing to them. I waited for Paul to get in touch, and gave him inward deadlines, telling myself if he didn't get in touch by Thursday, or by Saturday, I would get in touch myself. Time went by. I dithered, miserable, and meanwhile fixed up my French trip with Jilly and her twin brother Sam. We were going to travel by local buses, and camp as we went. When this was all arranged I rang Paul up at last to have a chat and let him know casually I was going; it took me ages to get the courage to dial, but the effort was wasted because Paul was away on some school project and though his mother said she'd tell him I rang when he got back, he did not contact me. I knew he was back because I saw him in the distance. The sight of him made my stomach lurch unpleasantly, and I hid in a doorway until the coast was clear. I was sure he hadn't seen me, and I was glad; I somehow had begun to be convinced that when I got back from Brittany everything would come right again, and any attempt at a meeting before then was doomed to failure. I did not think it out further; I busied myself in organizing the journey.

"Oughtn't you to write to your old friends and warn them you're going to be in Tréguinec at Whitsun?"

I stared in surprise at my mother. I hadn't thought of

Joël's family; I somehow imagined the little Breton resort would be full of strangers. "They'll all be in Paris. They won't be there."

"Don't be too sure. If you're on holiday, so might they be."

I didn't want to see any of them, I didn't want to create echoes of my old life there. "I'm only planning to stop in Tréguinec long enough to visit the grave. We're not going to camp there. We'll camp farther along the coast, there are some lovely places."

"It just occurred to me you might write to Joël's family."

"If I run into them, I run into them. Madame Joubert never liked me anyway, and I didn't like her either." Joël's family were no part of my pilgrimage. My mother frowned, but said no more. I began to wonder whether I ought to write, but never got round to it.

Jilly, Sam, and I took a ferry and then bus-hopped from village to town, working out a fairly direct route and enjoying ourselves very much. French buses vary a lot and are often full and noisy. It took us two days to get near Tréguinec, and then as we were going down the coast with a few miles left before we arrived, I made us all get off the bus. Sam and Jilly were aggrieved.

"Hey, we're nearly there. What's the matter with you?"

"This is a good place to camp. I'd forgotten it till we got here." I couldn't face Tréguinec without preparation. "And there's a super *crêperie* in the village. Come on, let's go there now, I'm famished." We bought the delicious thin pancakes which were a Breton specialty and ate them sitting on a wall. I had eaten pancakes on this wall before, on a visit with Joël and others to a dolmen. I felt very tense and odd. Faced with places I recognized, I wondered why on earth I'd come at all. I'll go to Tréguinec tomorrow sometime, I thought. There's no hurry.

The camp site was on a headland just above the beach, and there was a jetty from which local boys were fishing. It was a most attractive place altogether. There were masses of French on holiday, I noticed. That meant Tréguinec would be full of familiar faces. I absolutely couldn't meet them. I spent the next two days lazing with Sam and Jilly, until Jilly finally said: "We'll have to leave tomorrow afternoon if we're going to get back to catch the ferry. Aren't you going to Tréguinec at all?"

"I'll go tomorrow morning." There was no avoiding it. I could see from our headland the village of Tréguinec and the spire of the church where Joël was buried. The bell was tolling faintly; perhaps there was a Mass. After all, this was the week of Pentecost, *la Pentecôte*.

It happened that the next morning I woke very early indeed; dawn was just breaking. I felt very alert, and crawled carefully out of the tent taking care not to disturb the twins. I dressed quickly outside, and started to walk to Tréguinec. I took the empty main road; I decided to join the cliff path farther on.

I love walking along empty roads, and that morning was so fresh and clear that I found myself singing as I walked down the center of the road. I stopped that when I was nearly run over by a farm lorry, and walked more soberly but very happily along the verge. At last I was going, at last, at last.

Tréguinec had grown. There were new hotels and lots of new villas. I wondered if the café where I had so often played Ping-Pong was still run by a dear man called Jean. I turned inland along a small road before I came to the actual sea front; the road led uphill to the church past large shabby-looking villas with untidy gardens. Not far away

was the villa Joël's family owned. The Joubert family was
so big that the overflow had slept in a caravan behind the
house.

I walked quickly in the bright sunlight. It was now
about half past six, and I was ravenously hungry. In fact, I
was so hungry I felt quite lightheaded. I knew there was a
drinking fountain outside the church where I could get
some water, and this stopped the worst of my internal
rumblings.

I was there. I forced myself to walk into the churchyard. It was well cared-for and quite large. The church
door was open and I peeped in; there was a Mass in prog-
ress in a side chapel; I withdrew silently. I began to look
for Joël's grave.

It had never occurred to me that I would have trouble
finding it. I had visualized myself homing in on it, so I
didn't look for it very systematically. After a while I realized I had been down every path and still not found it. But
I *knew* he was buried here. I began to feel desperate. I also
did not want the priest to come and talk to me when he
came out of the Mass. If I was looking lost he might. I
rushed up and down, panicking.

How had I missed it. There it was: a vase of fresh
marigolds; a photograph in a permanent marble frame, the
same photograph I had been sent; a small white marble
cross, and on it:

JOËL CLÉMENT MARIE JOUBERT
*Mort à dixhuit ans*
1954–1972

*Repos eternel, donne à cil,*
*Sire, et clarté perpetuelle . . .*

François Villon

Joël had loved Villon best of all French poets. As I stared at this inscription, the top of my mind was only filled with how difficult Villon was, with his fifteenth-century French. *Clarté* was easy—light perpetual . . . but *cil?* . . . The solemn face stared out at me through thick protective glass. Joël, Joël. I was numb.

I heard footsteps; people were leaving after Mass. I wandered about, unwilling to be found near Joël. No one took any notice of me, and when they were all gone I went back. The marigolds were so fresh they cannot have been there very long; I was sure they must have been put there by one of the Jouberts; maybe by Suzanne, Joël's closest sister. I had liked her very much. I suddenly felt a great desire to see her, and his family again; why had I felt so against it, and left it so late? I would have to go down to their villa this morning and see them, if I was going to see them at all.

My stomach gurgled with hunger. I had enough francs for some breakfast; that was the first thing to take care of. I would go down to Jean's café and have some coffee and croissants, talk to my old friend and find out from him who was around in Tréguinec. Jean would know everything.

Without a backward glance, I hurried from the churchyard. It was now well after seven, not too early for Jean's café to be open, but early enough for the people I knew to be still in bed. I ran down the familiar hill, and there was the café unchanged, as shabby and comforting as ever. But it wasn't open yet. Jean must have changed his early morning habits.

I went down onto the beach; the tide was very high and the green water sparkled. I hadn't got my bathing things, but I waded in up to my thighs and gazed out over the sea. I remembered the hours and hours of fun I had had on this beach with Joël and my ache was piercing. My memory of him was fresh again; I could see, hear and sense him. If his hands had come over my eyes and his voice had said, *"Qui est?"* I would have laughed and turned round and splashed him with no sense of surprise.

A dog ran behind me barking, and its master appeared far down the beach. I stayed facing out to sea until he had passed, then I hurried back to the café. The door was now open. It was changed inside; the Ping-Pong table had gone and the bar had been tarted up in a half-hearted manner. But the place still smelled in the way only a French beach café can of Gauloises and coffee, sand and sea, orange juice and wine and dried wood. I sat down, scraping a chair noisily on the gritty boards. A woman appeared, fat and shiny and vaguely familiar. I ordered coffee and croissants, and I could see she found me familiar too. I asked if Jean was still around.

*"Mais oui.* But he's retired, he doesn't work so hard now. I manage the café."

I suddenly recognized her. "You're Laure, Jean's daughter."

"That's right." She frowned, trying to place me.

"I'm the English girl who used to come . . . Joël Joubert's friend."

She stared at me, said nothing for a moment, and then shouted through the door at the back of the bar.

*"Papa! Viens-ici! Depèche-toi!"* She was smiling delightedly. I heard rather slow footsteps and there was Jean. Thinner, older, stiffer, but my lovely friend Jean. He gave a roar when he saw me.

*"La petite Anglaise!"* He opened his arms and gave me a bone-cracking hug. There were tears in his eyes, and mine too. Jean had understood about Joël; how truly we had loved each other, and what it was like when he died. It was

too much seeing Jean again; he had believed in Joël and me. I cried on his shoulder until I was exhausted, and he cuddled me and patted me until I was calm. Then we both laughed.

"I told Laure you would come soon. I knew it."

I gazed at him wordlessly. It had never occurred to me to be expected. It had never occurred to me that someone else would think about us and care about us.

"I said, she'll come this summer. And there you are, at the best time of the day. Sit down, we'll have breakfast together."

We sat, and I felt shy and stiff as Laure put cups of coffee and croissants on the table.

"*Bon appétit.*"

I smiled at Jean's wrinkled face and kind eyes, and raised my cup to him.

"You're a bad girl. You've cut your beautiful hair short." He shook his head. "That lovely sheet of gold all gone. What a pity."

"I can grow it again any time. Tell me, Jean, who's around in Tréguinec? Are the Jouberts here?"

"They've sold their villa. You didn't know? They've gone. They have their holidays in the South now. They sold up the summer after your boy died."

Jean told me about the rest of my French friends, but it was Suzanne Joubert I had particularly wanted to see. I finished my cup of coffee and Jean went to get me another. I said I didn't have enough money for one and he looked pained.

"You do not pay for this breakfast. It is my pleasure." Laure's baby came toddling in and Jean gave her a piece of bread. I noticed a poster for a dance in the café, and it brought back more memories. Jean saw me looking at it.

"You will still be here next Saturday? You must come."

"I start back to England today. I'm camping with friends round the point."

"Ah. Mary. What a short visit." He looked disappointed; I felt guilty. I could easily have given him more time. We talked about this and that, but the café got busy and we were constantly interrupted. Also, I had to get back to Jilly and Sam before they started to worry. I began to take my leave, and Jean insisted on giving me a lift when he heard I planned to walk.

"Absolutely not. I take you on my 'phut-phut.'" His "phut-phut" was a battered scooter which took some time to start. When it finally did, Jean pulled his old cotton cap on more firmly and told me to hold tight. As we chuffed along, we shouted comments happily at each other, all constraint gone.

"*Et alors, ma petite Anglaise,* haven't you got a nice new boyfriend?"

"Not really." I could see him make a face of disbelief. "Well, I know a boy I like very much." Somehow it was easy to say these things in French. Paul. Paul. I should have sent that postcard instead of tearing it up.

"What's his name?"

"Paul."

"Don't be frightened of having a new boyfriend."

"I'm not frightened."

Jean squeezed his hooter vigorously at some cows wandering across the road. I looked at his funny hat and felt a great surge of affection for him. I knew it was either he or Laure who had put marigolds on Joël's grave.

When we puttered into the camp Jilly and Sam had packed up the tent and were sitting reading, drinking mugs of tea. They looked at me in surprise. I introduced Jean to them and he shook hands with both, his hat off. But he spoke no English, and their French was pretty basic, so it was a rather tongue-tied encounter. Jean put his hat back on and turned to me.

"Well, *ma petite Anglaise*, I must return to relieve Laure."

"Oh Jean, I can't tell you how good it has been to see you."

"I knew you would come, you see. Old Jean isn't stupid."

We hugged each other and kissed each other on both cheeks.

"You must promise me two things." He pinched my ear.

"What things?"

"You must grow your beautiful hair long again. And you must be kind and loving to this Paul. When pretty girls become hard it is not nice."

I stared into his blue eyes. "I'm not hard," I whispered.

"*Bien sûr*. What does an old man know?" He touched my chin with his finger, and then started to turn his "phut-phut." "*Au revoir*, Mary. Not *adieu*. I am sure you will come back again." I watched him bump his way out of sight, my heart full. I was sure it was *adieu*.

# *Trust*

## LYNNE REID BANKS

At the time of this story I was living in Canada. It was toward the end of the Second World War, and I was nearly sixteen—a rather uncomfortable mixture of child and woman, Canadian and English. My mother and I had been evacuated five years before to Saskatoon, Saskatchewan—euphemistically known as the Hub City of the Prairies—and had only during the last two grown accustomed to the flat sameness of the wheatfields, the vast space between towns broken by the stark, jutting grain elevators, white in the dry clear air.

We had even grown fond of Saskatoon itself; but it was always with relief that we escaped, during the baking hot months of the summer holidays, to one of the scattered lakes north of Prince Albert. Pushed like thumbprints into the all-but-unexplored Northern forests, the sheltered rims of these lakes accommodated occasional groups of log cabins in which farmers, woodsmen, and summer visitors shared the peace and beauty of the woods with the teeming wild life that belonged there.

In these magic surroundings we used to spend the long summer days in the open air, swimming and canoeing, walking, reading, or just lying dreaming in the sun. In the evenings the three-foot pine logs would burn with their blue flames and sweet smell, and we would sit and talk, listening to the piano students playing in the next cabin and the bitterns creaking in the reeds, or watch the fireflies, millions of them, dancing in the fringe of trees between our porch and the Lake, which was always a bright, luminous gray after the unbelievable sunset colors had faded.

That last summer before we returned to England was particularly enchanted. For one thing, I was in love for the first time. No one will ever convince me that one cannot be in love at fifteen. I loved then as never since, with all my heart and without doubts or reservations or artifice. Or at least, that is how I loved by the end of the summer. When we left for the Lake in June, it was all just beginning.

My boyfriend worked in Saskatoon, but the Lake was "his place"—the strange and beautiful wilderness drew him with an obsessive urgency, so I cannot claim it was only to see me that he got on his motorcycle as many Fridays as he possibly could, and drove three-hundred-odd miles along the pitted prairie roads to spend the weekend with us.

Sometimes he couldn't come, and then the joy would go out of everything until Monday, when I could start looking forward to Friday again. He could never let us know in advance, as we were too far from civilization to have a phone or even a telegraph service, so that it wasn't until noon on Saturdays that I had to give up hope. Three hundred miles in those conditions is quite a journey. Besides, Don was hard up, and sometimes worked overtime on weekends.

But except for those lost and empty Saturdays and Sundays, I was deliriously happy. So happy that I began to think, for the first time in years, quite a lot about God. After Don had managed to come for several consecutive weekends, I came to the conceited conclusion that God was taking personal care of me. I talked to Him as if to a companion, and somewhere in that maze of hot, contemplative days, when God, or nature, or whatever you care to call the abstract Power of the world, seemed almost tangibly close, I conceived the idea that if I posed a direct question the first answer that came into my mind would be the correct one.

The childishness of this faith game is easy to deride now; the fact remains that it worked. I used to try it out on simple things: "Will it rain tomorrow?" "Will there be a letter from England today?" and, most often of all, "Will Don come this week?" At first I used to be a little confused by the jumble of negative and affirmative thoughts that would rush through my mind, but after a while there would be a little space of whirling blankness, and then a yes or a no would flash forth quite clearly, and if it ever proved wrong, I don't remember it. Except for the last time.

One Monday morning I was sitting at the end of our little canoe jetty with one foot trailing in the warm water, watching the tiny fish prodding at it inquisitively with their transparent noses, when my mother came down to me, stepping over the gaping holes in the planking.

"Did you borrow a five-dollar bill out of my cashbox?" she asked.

"No . . ." I replied, stirring idly with my foot and watching the little fish flicker away.

"Funny," she said. "I must have put it somewhere else."

She went away, and I lay back on the planking, feeling it warm and rough through my shirt, and behind my sunbaked eyelids relived the past two days, moment by moment. After a while, my mother came back. Her hollow footsteps behind me had a worried urgency that made me sit up.

"I can't find it," she said. There was a little knot of muscles between her eyebrows.

"I'll come and help you look."

"It's no good," she said, pushing me back. "I remember now, I *did* put it in the box. There's nowhere else it could be."

"Well, what's happened to it?"

"I don't know," she said. She stood beside me, frowning across the bright, flat water.

I should explain that Don was not the only person who used to visit us. We had many friends, and weekends at the Lake during the heat of July were considered well worth the long train journey and the uncomfortable truck ride involved in reaching us. Lots of local people used to pop in too, as well as neighbors from nearby cabins. During the weekend just past, there had been a good half-dozen people on the premises besides Don.

I find it quite impossible to this day to understand why the thought that Don might have taken the five dollars should even have crossed my mind. But it did, and at once a cold pall of self-loathing fell on me. I shivered in the glittering heat, and my mother bent and put her arm round me.

"Don't worry, darling," she said. "We can't be sure anyone took it."

"But they're all friends," I mumbled. What had occurred to me would never in a hundred years have occurred to her; she would as soon have suspected *me* of stealing as Don. She said: "Anyone could have come in and taken it while we were over at the reef." But there were no strangers, and she knew it. The lakeside population is a tiny, isolated community, which no tramps or wanderers ever invade.

Five dollars was a respectable sum to us in those days, with only our meager allowance from England to live on. But my mother was never one to cry over spilled milk, and she told me to forget all about it.

But I couldn't. I think it was guilt at that flash of involuntary disloyalty that kept the thing alive in my mind. I hated myself for giving it a first thought, let alone a second, and as the days went by the silly, groundless suspicion grew, and my guilt with it, the one feeding the other. The happiness of our surroundings was utterly spoiled, and so was the former delight of forward-looking; I felt I couldn't look Don in the face again, and almost dreaded the coming weekend. And yet I could not shake off this feeling of doubt, which lay on my spirit like a guilty burden.

At first I refused to apply my newly found "test," because to do so would be to admit the doubt to myself, at a time when I was still desperately trying to pretend it was not there at all; and then, when I reached the stage of having to admit it, I was afraid to "ask" because I knew I would believe the answer.

But by Friday I was so wretched in my self-created hell that I could bear it no longer. I went away by myself onto the shore; the evening air was unusually heavy, and the placid water had an almost ominous beauty. I stood looking at the dying sunset, beyond the trees' ragged silhouette. It was beautiful—too beautiful for me, at that moment. I didn't feel fit to look at it. I started to cry in great, dry sobs, and suddenly I said aloud:

"Did Don take the five dollars?"

And the answer came quite clearly, "Yes."

The storm broke with the uncanny abruptness of all

weather changes in that land of extremes. One minute the accentuated reds and lemons of the sunset were smeared across the west; the next, the blackness of thunderclouds had obliterated them, and the leaden bowl of the sky was fissured with lightning which spread in infinite detail, like the veins of a leaf. It vanished, leaving me blinking in the sudden darkness; then came the thunder, and the next second the flat face of the Lake was dancing in angry peaks and the pines were lashing like whips.

I tried not to expect Don that night. I felt that my thoughts might have communicated themselves to him somehow, and that, sensing my treachery, he wouldn't come. But it was ironic that, convinced, irrationally, as I now was, of his guilt, I should nevertheless have longed to see him as I never had before.

I lay in bed under the sloping roof of the cabin and listened to the rain beating like multiple hammers over my head, feeling the wind shake the cabin to its foundations with one ferocious impact after another, watching the black square of window light up with blinding suddenness and frequency. Once I got up and stood looking out over the treetops, shivering; when the flashes came, they showed the solid forest swaying with the flexibility of a wheatfield.

I experienced a loneliness of spirit unequalled by anything I have felt since. My strange betrayal hurt in a sharp and basic way which would be impossible now, through the layers of self-protective insulation the years have laid on my heart.

I crawled back into bed, trying to close my throat against the tears. But when my mother, prompted by the sweet deep affinity between us, came in to me, she kissed my cheek and found it wet.

"Don't cry, sweetie," she said softly. "He may still come."

"I don't want him to!" I sobbed before I could stop my-self, and when, startled, she drew back and said, "But why?" I had to lie, and say it was because I was afraid for him, riding through the storm over bad roads which the rain would now have reduced to sheets of yellow mud.

When she had tucked me in and gone, the lie became true. I lay thinking about the very real danger of those roads . . . you couldn't walk along them safely after heavy rain; your feet would slip from under you on the crude camber. Would he have enough sense to stop and wait until the storm ended? But the roads in Northern Canada are not like the friendly well-populated English ones, where there is always a town or at least a farmhouse within walking distance. You can travel a hundred miles with nothing but the rough road itself to show that you are not the first human being to go that way.

I imagined Don fighting the storm, unwilling to stop in the middle of some sodden wilderness. The strength of the wind buffeting the cabin made the motorbike, which had always looked to me so heavy and solid, seem in my fright-ened thoughts frail enough to be blown onto its side by the first gust that struck it. I thought of Don pinned under it, skidding, his face pressed into the yellow clay; I saw the rain beating onto the stillness of his young neck above his leather jacket; I heard the coughing of the disabled ma-chine above the fury of the storm.

It was hours later, when I had relived the scene a hun-dred times, that I suddenly realized the sound of the roar-ing engine was real. The storm was dying; the wind was no more than a sullen, spasmodic growl through the trees and a steady patter of rain on the roof. I lay absolutely still, re-lief and panic fighting for ascendancy within me, each in itself overwhelming enough to freeze the breath in my lungs as I heard Don's heavy, tired footsteps on the wooden stairs.

He stood in the open doorway. The faint early-dawn light from the window gleamed on his wet black hair, his wet face and the streaming, shiny jacket. He stood for a long moment, his breath laboring, not knowing whether I was awake or asleep. His arms hung wearily at his sides; I could make out his stooped shoulders and hear the faint tapping as water ran off him onto the plank floor.

Then I whispered to him, and stretched out my hand. He came and bent over me, pressing his cold wet face against my hot one. The rain from his hair dripped onto my pillow. He tried to keep my hands under the bed-clothes, saying, "No, you'll get so wet—" laughing under his breath, holding my hands down with one hand and try-ing to struggle out of his soaking jacket. But I got free and threw my arms round his neck, pulling him down to me, and he gave in. I felt the wet stiffness of the jacket through my thin pajamas; his hands, freezing cold, held me close; his icy wet ear was against my cheek, his lips pressed to my shoulder . . . The guilt and the doubt broke up all at once within me, the way the solid surface of the frozen Sas-katchewan River breaks up in the spring. The released water rushes along, carrying its broken bonds of ice along in a crashing torrent. That was the sort of *exulting* freedom I felt now I knew the absolute stupidity of my fears.

Most truths are learned gradually, through many small lessons. But the truth about love—or one of the truths, for there are many, and none is absolute except for the person for whom it is real—came rushing in on me in that wet, close, relieving moment. It was this: that it isn't until you have truly doubted someone that you can truly and finally believe in them.

"Don—" I whispered, into his cold ear, all my recent fear in my voice.

"Fathead," he whispered back tenderly. "You know I can drive Matilda through an earthquake . . . Go to sleep." He dried my face with a distant corner of the sheet, turned my pillow over to the dry side, and tucked the bedclothes snugly round me. My hands kept creeping out to touch him, and he kept firmly pushing them back into the warmth. "Close your eyes," he ordered. When I did, the long exhaustion swept over me blackly. I fell asleep halfway through his kiss.

The next morning the sun shone brilliantly from a cloudless sky. The Lake was a sheet of luminous glass, and every pine needle glistened in its cleanness like a shred of green silk. From the earth rose an overwhelming smell of bruised freshness.

The three of us sat on the wired-in porch and drank our morning coffee, watched our almost-tame chipmunks rejoicing on the steaming woodpile, and laughed at the awfulness of the night behind us. My mother, too, it seemed, had lain awake letting her imagination run riot until she heard Don arrive. And the drive, for all Don's pretended nonchalance, had been no pleasure trip.

"Was it raining when you left Saskatoon?" I asked, and when he said it had been, heaven's hardest, I burst out, "Oh, then why did you come? You needn't have. It was too dangerous . . ."

He pooh-poohed this, and repeated that Matilda could weather the raging Atlantic if she had to. "Besides," he added after a moment, "I *had* to come this weekend."

Before I could ask why, my mother asked us if we'd walk up to the store for the groceries. It was a rhetorical question; we were holding hands and looking at each other, and she could see it didn't matter to us what we did, so long as we were together. She went into the living room to collect money and her shopping list. While she was gone, I noticed that Don's eyes had black rings under them; the expression on his face was sober and grown-up. He started to tell me something and then kissed me instead, leaning across the coffee cups. The sun was blissfully warm on my closed eyelids and on our clasped hands.

My mother called me. Her voice had a funny note in it.

I went in to her. My eyes, unused to the darkness inside the cabin, could not see how she looked; but she was holding the moneybox.

"Look," she said, holding it out to me.

Inside, lying on top of some one-dollar bills and small change, was another bill for five dollars.

"It's back!" I exclaimed. "How funny! When do you suppose that could have happened?"

"It wasn't there last night," she said. She sounded as if her throat were dry.

I laughed at her. "What nonsense!" I said. "It must have been. Nobody's been in the house since last night, except us and Don. I'll bet it's been there the whole time." She didn't answer, and I went on: "Well, come on, let's have the list and we'll be off before it gets too hot."

She handed me the list in silence, and then picked out the five-dollar bill. She held it a moment, as if in doubt about giving it to me; impatient to get back to Don I almost grabbed it from her hand, kissed her, and ran back onto the sun-flooded porch.

Don had his back to me. He was hunched up a little, staring with concentration into his empty coffee cup. As I stood looking down at him, feeling the sun's warmth glowing on my skin like a blessing, I thought: to love someone is lovely, but incomplete. It's trust that rounds love out, making it perfect. I thought of my child's asking game, and shrugged tolerantly at myself as I had been yesterday. I had the answers to all the questions now.

I dropped a kiss on the smooth black head. "Come on," I said. "I've got five dollars. Let's go buy the world."

# *Fireworks for Elspeth*

## RUMER GODDEN

When Elspeth woke on the last morning she was visited by a feeling of extraordinary simplicity; everything she had to do was done; there was nothing now but to go. She felt as if the doors and windows of the house were already wide open, with the sun shining on its white walls, on the lawns and the lavender bushes; the sun seemed to make a path from her own window over the lawn and the tops of the trees, over the copse to the wood and the sky; yes, it looked like a path. I have only to go, thought Elspeth blissfully. Roderick, her black cocker spaniel, lay at the foot of her bed; there it was, it was true, a gap in her mind where she must say goodbye to Roderick—but that was legitimate grief, thought Elspeth, nothing disturbing. Nothing disturbing, she thought and stretched herself on the bed; then she remembered the lunch party.

How she had pleaded with Mother! "A lunch party! Oh *Mother*, no! Please no."

"Why not?"

"It wouldn't be—suitable," Elspeth had said, with temerity.

"Elspeth, do I or do I not know what is suitable? *Not* a party! Just the family and a few intimate friends."

"But they are the worst."

"Elspeth!"

Elspeth would have liked to have said, it's the questions and the looks. I feel the looks, Mother. I know I shouldn't feel them but—but I do and they talk so much. They—they prise everything open. Aunt Euphrosyne and Morna and Jean, Lady Bannerman, all of them. They know me so well they take it for granted they can ask things but . . . they have such picking eyes, thought Elspeth in despair. They pick everything to pieces, into little little pieces; this is whole, in me, but they tatter it to pieces. I know it is my fault to let them, but they do. "Mother," she had begun but Mother was saying, "Just Aunt Euphrosyne and Uncle Arthur and Morna and Jean. Major Fitzgerald, of course . . ."

"And the Baldocks and Lady Bannerman and Larry and Colin Crump," said Elspeth bitterly.

"They are exactly whom I thought of asking," said Mother; then she had looked at Elspeth and her face hardened. "Well, Elspeth, why not?"

Elspeth could never say things to Mother; she could have talked to Aunt Bevis but that would have made Mother worse. "Bevis is *not* your mother," Mother often said.

"It—it will all be so complicated," Elspeth had said, about the lunch party, stumbling over the words. "I—I wanted it simple, quiet and—kind of—usual, Mother." She picked up Roderick and held him tightly to give herself courage while Mother tapped with a pencil on the blotter. "Don't you understand, Mother?"

"No," said Mother.

"I thought—if I could leave, just simply, as if it were everyday . . ."

"You *cannot* pretend," said Mother, "that this kind of thing is everyday."

That had stopped Elspeth, and she could not bear to have this same scene again; instead she had said desperately, "Think of the washing-up. Father and I shall have to leave at half past two. I shan't be here to help Marlowe."

"We shall have to get used to that." Mother's voice had been cold. "I shall get Mrs. Paget from the village," and she had picked up her pen. "It will be easiest for everybody. If you thought at all, Elspeth, you would know what these last few hours will be like for us; for your father and me, though I must say Father doesn't seem to feel it; *if* you thought, but of course you don't think, if you did, you couldn't do this."

"Oh *Mother!*" Elspeth had pleaded once again but Mother held up her hand for silence, that thin white peremptory hand that looked fragile and was strong—strong as iron. Elspeth knew how strong it was and her nerves tingled. It was almost time to go but she had not gone yet; she could still be stopped. The hand was heavy with rings; Mother always wore her rings; diamonds, rubies, sapphires. Her hand must be strong to bear those rings, thought Elspeth, and she wondered idly what she herself would have done with them when, as Mother had often said they should, they came to her. Now they won't, Elspeth had thought, with relief. No rings, no Lady Bannerman's emeralds, none of the family silver and pictures and china. Daphne will have them all. I—I have escaped, thought Elspeth and her face glowed; she was filled with this inner contentment, this feeling of rightness that was hers now by right—or almost hers—as if it had been given to me, thought Elspeth, and she thought, it is my gift from God, my jewels and money, my family.

Mother had returned to the subject of the luncheon

party. "It will be best," she said, "no matter what I feel—
and it doesn't matter what I feel—be quiet, Elspeth. I won't
have people saying we're bundling you off. They might
think there was something wrong, a family rift—or that
there was an unhappy love affair."

"Couldn't they think it was choice?" asked Elspeth. At
that, Mother had bowed her head and her neck stiffened as
it did when she was mortally displeased; she pulled her
chair into the writing table and began to write the notes,
but her hand trembled on the paper and Elspeth, watching,
was smitten. Once again she had hurt Mother—for—for
nothing, thought Elspeth. When I'm so happy why can't I
be generous? Why must I always do it? she thought in despair; do what Sister Monica so often said she must not,
seek her own way? Trying to impose her own will, instead
of accepting? "In these last few days try to do, to be, everything your parents want," Sister Monica had said.
"Show them how you love them . . ." and I can't be five
minutes with Mother before we begin . . . No wonder
they wonder at me, thought Elspeth. This rebellious and
unpleasant girl to make a nun!

She had looked helplessly across the room at Aunt Bevis
who had been sewing in the window and Aunt Bevis had
looked back at her and smiled. Never, thought Elspeth,
had anyone as clear eyes as Aunt Bevis—they were set a little tilted as if, for all her quietness, Aunt Bevis had an extra
private and particular view of the world. Is that what
makes her so—large? thought Elspeth now, so without
walls? She can see over the wall—but then Mother had
caught the look and asked sharply, "Bevis, where's the list?
You took it when you went to the telephone. Now it's
*lost*."

"It's under the blotter on the right-hand side," said Aunt
Bevis. "Thursday, 2nd April, at a quarter to one," Mother

had written in her clear, pointed hand. On Thursday, 2nd April, today thought Elspeth in bed, she, Elspeth Catherine Mary Erskine, was to enter the Order of the Sisters of Mary at their Convent of St. Faith at Chiswick where she had already spent two retreats. She was very happy about it; very shy, but no one seemed to grasp that she was either of these things.

"What are you going to be called?" her cousin Morna had asked.

"Reverend Mother had agreed that I shall be Catherine Mary," said Elspeth. "They are saints' names as well as my own."

"Sister Catherine Mary." Morna tried it, and relapsed into helpless giggles.

"Shut up, Morna!" said her sister Jean but Morna could not shut up. Soon Jean and then Elspeth herself were giggling too, as they had always giggled all their short lives when they were together.

"Really! You girls are too silly," Aunt Euphrosyne always said, but the silliness broke out as soon as they met, though Morna was twenty to Elspeth's and Jean's nineteen.

"But a nun *isn't* funny," Elspeth had protested, shaking helplessly.

"Of c-course not," said Jean. "It's just—you—one of us—as a n-nun!"

The giggling had been all right, it was silly but easy; it was the questions, the—feeling against her, that Elspeth could not face. I wish I belonged to another family, she thought that often in these days, one of those families, in Ireland or America, where it's part of family life for a daughter or a sister or cousin to enter an Order. In ours you would think no one in the world had ever joined an Order before. "They make it seem so extraordinary," she said bitterly to Sister Monica, who was Mistress of the

Novices. "If only I could *tell* them, Sister. If only I could explain."

"Wait," said Sister Monica. "Wait and they will see."

For a long time now people had been exhorting Elspeth to wait. "Sixteen is too young. Don't be ridiculous." "Seventeen's too young." Elspeth had retorted with St. Thérèse of Lisieux, as young girls wanting to marry have retorted with Juliet. "St. Thérèse was a case apart," she was told. "Wait," and, "Eighteen is too young. Wait."

She had, of course, needed her parents' consent and at one time it seemed that Mother, and Father led on by Mother, never would consent. Then at long last there was hope, but she still had to wait. "If, at the end of a year you still want it . . ."

"I shall still want it," said Elspeth.

"You always were obstinate," said Mother. "Even as a little thing you would rather be sent to bed or shut up in the cloakroom than give in."

The trouble is, thought Elspeth, that I have always given in—except over this. Now I can't. She did not understand how she managed to be so steady but, when the year was up, they had given their consent—if Mother's could be called a consent. Even when it was decided, Mother never left Elspeth alone. "Robert killed, Daphne gone, one might think you would realize that you are all we have left."

"But Mother, you didn't mind when Daphne went away to be married. Hong Kong is the other side of the world!"

"That was *quite* different," said Mother. "Marriage is a woman's destiny."

"But Mother . . ."

"I hope I should never be so selfish as to stand between my child and *that*," said Mother.

"But Mother . . ."

"If only I could have seen you happily married," said Mother.

"But Mother, there are other . . ."

"Husband, home, children," said Mother.

"Mother, if I were marrying a king or a prince . . . !"

It was of no use. Mother would not listen and if she had, Elspeth could not have explained.

The news had burst suddenly on the family and the family friends. Usually, over any happening or idea, Mother took Aunt Euphrosyne and most of the neighborhood into her strict confidence—how often had Robert and Daphne and Elspeth writhed when their most private doings and feelings were made discreetly and unfailingly public. Now, until the ultimate decision was taken, Mother had not breathed a word. I suppose she thought it would spoil my chances, thought Elspeth. Young men should shy off me if they knew. I mightn't get all my dances! Now young men, dances, chances, did not matter. The news was out and everyone seemed bewildered.

"But how did it happen?" asked Mr. Baldock.

"It began when she went on that wretched French family exchange holiday," said Mother. "The daughter . . ."

Yes, there, with Jeanne Marie, thought Elspeth. Dear, dear Jeanne Marie.

"In Paris, that's where she got the idea," Mother complained.

"What a place to go to and get the idea of being a nun," said Mr. Baldock.

Mr. Baldock, a mild little man who grew violets, was Elspeth's godfather and now he looked at her as if he had been given a little seedling to cherish and it had suddenly grown into a rampant vine. "Can't *you* get this nonsense out of her head?" Elspeth had heard him ask Aunt Bevis.

"Is nonsense the right word?" asked Aunt Bevis.

"Well, no," said Mr. Baldock. "But Elspeth! Our pretty little girl!"

"She's not a little girl," said Aunt Bevis.

"It seems so unnatural," said Mr. Baldock. "Elspeth dear, are you sure?"

The family were more definite.

"She's out of her mind!" said Uncle Arthur.

"Girls get like this," said Aunt Euphrosyne. "It's usually anemia."

"Elspeth is not the *least* anemic," said Mother. "She has a lovely color," and she began to cry. "She's serious, Euphy."

"I can't believe it," said Aunt Euphrosyne. "Elspeth! Not *Elspeth!* Why she was always the naughty disobedient one."

"Euphy is glad, of course," said Mother afterwards. "She was always jealous because you were by far the prettiest."

"Mother, don't, don't say things like that!"

"It's true. At least you'll be out of the way," said Mother vindictively. "I expect she thinks that now Larry will marry Jean."

There had been something a little sadistic about the cousins.

"They give you all the worst things to do when you're a novice," said Morna. "You scrub floors and clean lavatories and shovel coal. You do all the rough work."

"And you won't like that," said Aunt Euphrosyne. "You were always what Nanny calls backward in coming forward to help."

"Was I?" asked Elspeth. She did not really, fairly think she was.

"Last time you stayed with us," said Morna, "you left

your towel on the bathroom floor and the tiles were all over powder and you never even turned down your bed."

"They bully you and humiliate you to find out what you're made of. I have read about it," said Jean and she added, "If you like one thing more than another, it's taken away."

"Life does that to you as well," said Aunt Bevis. "As you will find out."

Elspeth had looked at Aunt Bevis in surprise. Aunt Bevis's cheeks had been quite pink.

The whole neighborhood was roused.

"A well-plucked girl like that!" said Major Fitzgerald. "You should have seen the way she rode that mare of mine in the Dunbar Hunt Cup, not anyone's ride, I can tell you."

Colin Crump had blinked at Elspeth from behind his glasses and something seemed to boil up in him as if he wanted to speak; of course, no one counted Colin Crump, but there was trouble with Larry.

"I thought you were going to marry Larry," said Lady Bannerman in her gruff voice and she said, as Elspeth thought she would, "I meant to give you my emeralds."

Elspeth was touched and went to kiss her but Lady Bannerman held her off. "Don't kiss me," she said; there was a harshness in her voice that smote Elspeth. "You hurt Larry," said Lady Bannerman, her lips trembling. "You led him on, you little—vixen!"

"I didn't," Elspeth had said that before she could stop herself. "Don't answer. Be quiet. Submit," said Sister Monica, but Elspeth was cut. Led Larry on! She might have said, "He was there before I led him," but that would have been to hurt him even more. She had picked up Roderick and hid her face against him and immediately all thought of Larry was wiped away. Soon, soon, Elspeth had thought, I shall have to say goodbye to you, Roddy. Roddy's small black spaniel body was warm, silky, firm in her arms. He licked her neck and his eyes, between his absurd down-hanging ears, looked into her face. Her own eyes swam in sudden tears. She dared not keep Roderick in her arms; hastily she put him down.

"You're not listening to me," Lady Bannerman had said. "Hard as hails. You young things don't care how much you hurt."

They all said that but, willy nilly, thought Elspeth, she had to put on this front of hardness with them, or give way completely. "She's grown so hard," they said.

"Father is twelve years older than I," said Mother. "When he goes, I shall be left alone. If I get ill . . ."

"Mother, why should you get ill? You're awfully strong."

"You're like marble," said Mother, "like marble."

I'm not. I'm not. If only I were! thought Elspeth, and she had thought of Jeanne Marie who was already professed and of Jeanne Marie's father and mother and brother who were so glad. Elspeth had borrowed the old Rover from Father and gone over to Chiswick to find Sister Monica. "Sister, ought I to give it all up?"

"You must ask yourself that," said Sister Monica. All the Sisters were the same; when you asked them, implored them, knelt to them, they put you gently back on your own feet.

Elspeth had looked up at Sister Monica's calm face. Sister Monica was sorting beans into bags for the kindergarten school; the infants used them for counting and Elspeth watched her fingers, picking the beans up in twenties, never making a mistake and slipping them into bags and tying the string with a firm knot.

"Sister, help me," said Elspeth.

"Dear child, I can't help you," but perhaps Sister Monica had spoken to Mother Dorothea because the Reverend Mother had sent for Elspeth.

"If you have the least doubt, Elspeth . . ."

"I haven't Reverend Mother." There Elspeth was firm; then the firm clearness clouded. "It's not my doubts, it's theirs. They make me wonder if I'm selfish. Mother, what should I do?"

"I think you should read the Commandments," said Mother Dorothea.

"The—the Commandments?"

"Yes. They are in the right order."

Now Elspeth understood. Her firmness shone but she cried, "If only I could *explain* to them, Mother. If I could make them see. I—I'm so dumb!"

Reverend Mother was silent for a few moments and then she said, "Perhaps you are given no words because there is no need for words. The action speaks, Elspeth," and she asked, her face serious, "Isn't that the way of the Cross?"

"But—but mine is such a little thing," said Elspeth, slightly shocked.

"A little thing but it makes you suffer. I think you have to consent to suffer, Elspeth. If Our Lord had not consented, He would have spoiled God's plan; have you thought of that? On the Cross He did simply what was asked of Him. He did not try and improve on the work of the Master. He used no fireworks," brought out Mother Dorothea after a hesitation.

Fireworks. That was a funny word for Reverend Mother to use, Elspeth had thought. It seemed almost irreverent. She sat silent, thinking, then she said, "But . . ." and remembered it was not customary to argue with Reverend Mother.

"But what? You may speak, Elspeth."

"The sky darkened," pleaded Elspeth, "the veil was—rent."

Reverend Mother was adamant. "That was given Him," said Reverend Mother. "Sometimes things are given; it's not for us to expect or ask. No. He did not use His power." Her voice grew deep with feeling. "They taunted Him and crowned Him with thorns. They told Him to come down off the Cross and prove Himself God and how did He answer? He let them win; hung there and died." Reverend Mother's face became marvelously kind and she put her hand on Elspeth's head. "He didn't ask for vindication but suffered and died—and lived. That proved Him God."

As Elspeth drove home it had stayed in her mind; she had thought about it every day since.

The second of April remained fixed. Mother's invitations went out and were accepted and the time went quickly till it came to the last day and Elspeth woke now to that sensation of emptiness and space, the windows and doors open and the sun streaming in. On the borderland of her sleep the birds sounded like the Convent choir where the children chirruped in an unconscious cherubic singing; she opened her eyes and looked along the sun's path that seemed to go from her bed, across the garden and the tops of the trees, across the copse where she used to play with Robert, to the woods and the far sky. The path might, she thought, have been a vision, only it was the sun; the singing might have been cherubs, only it was the birds; and suddenly, feeling completely happy and rational, she sat up in bed.

Aunt Bevis came in with two cups of tea. In her old Paisley dressing gown she sat down on the bed. "Well, I must say," said Aunt Bevis, "it's refreshing to go away without packing."

In the past weeks Elspeth had given all her things away; her books in the white bookcase, the doll Mignonette she had had since she was five, and Dinah, her old rubbed velvet pickaninny; all her clothes, shoes, ornaments, treasures, had gone. The gardener's children had some of her things, the cousins some. "Would Morna like my pink net dress?" "Jean, my tennis racket's for you. What a pity you can't get into my boots." The riding boots were new, glossy, black on their trees. Major Fitzgerald had given them to Elspeth for her birthday. "Fifty-six guineas," the Major said, mournfully.

"I couldn't warn him," said Elspeth. "Mother wouldn't let me."

As she gave away her things, her happiness mounted— until other people came in. "Mother, would you and Father mind if I gave my brushes to Marlowe? I mean—she's been with us so long and she thinks they're lovely."

"You thought them lovely once," said Mother.

"I—I do now. Of course I do. I love them but I won't need them," said Elspeth.

I won't need anything, I shall be free. That was all done. This heavenly morning she was empty of things and she lay back in bed as she thought: no more fittings and bringing things back on approval and thinking what I shall wear: and my face, with its horrible freckles, won't matter: my hair and Mother wanting it to be waved and having it cut only by Mr. Charles: and not wearing the same dress twice in the same place—and new hats and having things shortened and taken in and cleaned, and washing out gloves and handkerchiefs . . . "No, not even packing," said Elspeth aloud. The new life was breaking through the old but for this last day it had to be an admixture; in each thing, in each thought, there was both old and new.

After Aunt Bevis had gone, Elspeth dressed. It was the

last time she would put on these clothes, usual clothes; a gray skirt, gray blouse, pale pink jersey, stockings, gray shoes. They would do for the lunch party. At the Convent she would take them off and pack them in a cardboard box and give it to Sister Monica.

"What will you wear?" Morna had asked. Morna and Jean were terribly curious about every detail. The Order wore a plain black habit. "Like a rather full black dress but long," said Elspeth, "and black stockings and shoes."

"Wool stockings, flat shoes?" asked Morna.

"Yes," said Elspeth and Morna made a face. "Go on," said Morna. "Tell some more."

"We wear a white toque."

"Is that the head thing?"

"Yes. For six months I'm on probation. Then I'm a novice for two years. Then I change the white veil for a black and am a Junior for three more. I'm given a black cord with a crucifix," said Elspeth.

"What will you wear at night?" asked Jean.

"A nightgown, I suppose," said Elspeth.

"Don't you know?"

"I didn't ask," said Elspeth, suddenly shy.

"She took it for granted, I expect," said Aunt Bevis and she rounded on Jean. "What do you think she will wear? A black shroud?"

Aunt Bevis had promised to take Elspeth's few remaining things and send them away with her Relief Committee box.

"You had better wait six months, Bevis," Mother had said. "She has six months in which to change her mind."

"Mother, I shan't change my mind."

"No, you won't," said Mother and she said bitingly, "What is the use of hoping when there isn't any hope?"

That was one of the times when Elspeth had timidly approached her.

"Mother, if only you could be glad!"

"Glad!" and for the first time she had said to Elspeth, "What *is* it that draws you Elspeth? What is it you see? I wish I could understand."

Elspeth took heart and cast about for words. "It's as if instead of being blown about with life, with all the days and years," Elspeth said or tried to say, "you were rooted whole in a whole place."

"But you have a place, a good home," said Mother.

"Yes, but . . ." "There are pieces in a kaleidoscope, bits of paper and rag; you twist the glass and they are whole in a whole pattern." She might have used that symbol, or "It's like finding yourself on a map, knowing where you are, and then you know the direction"; but Elspeth could only twist her hands helplessly.

"It was that horrid little Jeanne Marie," said Mother.

"It wasn't," said Elspeth hotly. Then she tried painfully for the exact truth. "It wasn't only Jeanne Marie. She was only a little part. Why, it was always," said Elspeth with sudden light. "Why Mother, you taught me. Think. Think of hymns," said Elspeth.

"Hymns?"

"Don't you remember how you used to play and we sang?"

"Oh yes," said Mother, softening, "on Sunday evenings."

They both remembered those mild evenings.

"There was that one," said Elspeth. " 'Loving Shepherd of Thy Sheep.' "

Mother's eyes filled with tears. "It was Robert's favorite hymn."

"But think of what it meant," said Elspeth impatiently, "what it said. Didn't you *mean* us to take it seriously?"

Mother's eyes had flickered. "Seriously but not too seriously," Mother would have said, if she were truthful, but she could not very well say that; instead she had said bitterly, "I never thought I should have to suffer by your being good!" and Elspeth had sighed. All the scenes ended like that.

There were sausages for breakfast. The table was laid with a white cloth, blue and white china, silver, a bowl of primroses. The coffee bubbled gently in the Cona; there was a smell of coffee, hot milk, sausages, toast, marmalade and apples. "What will they give you to eat in that place?" Marlowe had often asked. Marlowe was worried about that; she had wanted Elspeth to take a bottle of malt and cod-liver oil. "But I couldn't, Marlowe dear." At any rate Marlowe was determined that Elspeth should eat one last good breakfast. Morna and Jean, too, often talked about the food.

"You'll have lentils," said Morna, "and fish. Ugh!"

"Bread and water on Fridays," said Jean.

"No, on Fridays you'll fast, and what about Lent?"

"Listen," said Aunt Bevis. "Have you ever seen a nun who didn't look perfectly well fed?" When they came to think about it, as a matter of fact, they had not.

Mother's breakfast tray was there. "I'll take it up," said Elspeth and Aunt Bevis did not interfere.

Mother was sitting up in bed reading her letters.

"Your breakfast, Mother."

"Why didn't you let Marlowe bring it?"

"I wanted to," said Elspeth and kissed her. Mother did not say anything sharp and by her bed, on the table, was Elspeth's miniature Dresden cup and saucer. Elspeth had brought it to her, the last of her things. Never, thought

Elspeth, had she loved people as much, as—as compassionately as when she gave away her possessions. "Mother, will you have this?" and she put the little rosy cup, with its shepherds and shepherdesses, down at Mother's side.

Mother had not answered but now she had it by her bed, and again Elspeth felt that trembling love. She bent down and kissed her mother. "Remember I—I love you just as much," she whispered.

Mother sighed. "That's some consolation." They were, in that moment, closer than they had ever been; then Mother put up her hand to Elspeth's cheek, the rings felt cold and hard. Mother sighed again, then she said, turning over her letters, "Will they let you have your own post?"

Elspeth was startled. "I—I don't know, Mother. I never asked. I don't see why not."

"Those places are full of taboos," said Mother. "I'm not going to write letters and have them pruned by the Sister Superior."

"I suppose they know best for us, Mother." Elspeth said that tactlessly, but she was trying to convince herself. Mother flushed and said something that linked straight with what Mother Dorothea had said, though Mother would have hated to know that.

"Honoring your father and your mother is a commandment," said Mother and she gave a harsh laugh, "but of course it's a long way down the list."

Things are made clear at least, thought Elspeth, quite and horridly clear, but she could not bear it; she said as she had often said when she had had to go back to school, "Mother, don't. Don't. Not on my last day."

After a moment Mother said in a normal everyday voice, "What are you going to do this morning?" and Elspeth answered as she had answered a thousand times, "Oh, all the usual things."

But that was not quite true; after she had helped with the work, she planned to go all round the house and garden and into the copse, with Father perhaps, and take Roderick for a last scamper in the woods. That's what I want to do, thought Elspeth. I want to see the house for the last time, the old white walls, the flagged path, the lavender bushes, the slated roof brooding among the trees. I shall see it again, of course, but I shall be separated, not quite as I am now. She had meant to go all over it, inside as well as out, touch each window sill, see it all: the gleam of silver and copper and brass, the polished mahogany, the white sheepskin rug in front of the drawing-room fire: the crystal vases of cut daffodils, the books and papers, *Punch* and *The Times* folded in the paper rack: the worn red brocade on the seats of the chairs: the patterned staircarpet, the wallpaper in the bedrooms, the Peter Rabbit frieze in the nursery and its window bars and high fender; she had meant to go into the copse and see if the wild hyacinths, that she used to pick with Robert, were out; she had meant to walk down the wood paths with Roderick, but there was the lunch party, of course.

Elspeth dusted the drawing room and put out extra ashtrays and then helped Aunt Bevis with the flowers. Mother was even more fussy than usual about the flowers.

"What would *you* like on the table, Elspeth? It's your party." That had become true. Mysteriously it had become Elspeth's party. "Of course I would do anything for you children," Mother said, pushing back her hair and smoothing her forehead where, obviously, she had a headache, "but these days the work *is* heavy. I had thought of primroses," said Mother, returning to the flowers.

"Primroses would be lovely," but when the primroses were done, Mother remembered the pudding was white and the whole effect would be pale. "It will look hideous, quite hideous in this dark room; you must get brightly colored primulas." Elspeth picked them, orange and rust primulas, dark crimson, vivid blue and magenta, and arranged them in a great bowl.

There were the best tablemats to get out, the lace in one was creased and had to be ironed; there were finger bowls to wash; she had to go down to the village for cigarettes, though she would have liked to keep out of the village. "You go off today then, Miss Elspeth," and when Elspeth said, "Yes," they all avoided her eyes and looked embarrassed; all except the postmistress, Mrs. Cox, who was jauntily confident she would come back. The Post Office was also the village shop. Elspeth had to face Mrs. Cox. "You will soon have enough of it," she told Elspeth as she handed her the cigarettes. "We shall soon have you back." Elspeth did not argue as she did with Mother; she knew she was a nine days' wonder in the village and she made her hasty escape.

When she came in, the telephone was ringing and she went to answer it. "Hullo," said Elspeth and the voice at the other end paused before it spoke. "Is that—you, Elspeth?" it said, uncertainly. "Could I speak to your mother?" Since they heard that Elspeth was going to be a nun, their friends seemed to doubt that she could answer the telephone; but nuns telephone, thought Elspeth in irritation; they use typewriters and vacuum cleaners and go in cars and airplanes. They drive cars; I have even seen a nun driving a buggy very fast; they are not medieval idiots, thought Elspeth.

Everybody's nerves were getting overtaxed. Mother went to lie down, even Aunt Bevis was cross and Marlowe, in the kitchen, was unapproachable. I didn't mean it to be like this, thought Elspeth unhappily; she looked across the lawn, where the daffodils were bending and bobbing along the hedge by the wicket gate that led into the copse; she could see the tops of the birch trees, the milk gleam of their stems, but time was getting short and she had to help Marlowe make the pudding. It was one of Mother's favorites, mushrooms in grass; the mushrooms were meringue shells, lined with chocolate and turned upside down on fondant stems; they stood on a base of chocolate mousse decorated with fronds of angelica grass. While Elspeth was arranging them in the pantry her father came in and stood by her. He watched while she cut the angelica grass and wearily stuck it in. "Damned flummery," said Father suddently.

"Dad, I wanted to come with you and see what they are doing in the copse," said Elspeth miserably.

He jingled his keys and the silver in his pockets. "The heavy timber's gone," he said, "except the big beech. It took two days to get that down. I should like you to have seen it. Fine tree!" then he added, "Better do as your Mother wants."

Father never made an outcry. "Your Mother's a very emotional woman," he had often said to his children. "She feels." Her feelings were so strong that no one paid much attention to his. When Robert was killed, Mother collapsed but Father only seemed more silent, to grow a little smaller, a little balder; he began to have indigestion, but he was quiet and gentle as before. Daphne was his favorite but when she married Cyril, and that had meant Hong Kong, he had only been anxious about her settlement; he had had to sell some of the land, some of his first editions, and take off some of the timber as he was doing now in the copse, but he never spoke of bills or worries, except perhaps about the bullfinches that had invaded the fruit last summer; he only took more soda mints. Nowadays, thought Elspeth, he always smelled of soda mints.

When Elspeth had made her decision, he had said, "You really want to do this, Kitten?"

"Yes, Dad."

He looked at her more seriously than she had known that he could look. "You know what it means?"

"Yes."

"The privations, Elspeth, and the—deprivations."

"Yes. Reverend Mother has explained them clearly"—Elspeth might have said, 'terribly clearly'—"to me."

"I shall have to sell out some shares," said Father. Elspeth was smitten and he said, "Don't look worried. If you had married, you would have had to have had a settlement," and he put his hand on her shoulder and said what none of them had said, "This calls for something handsome."

Elspeth, flushed and incoherent with gratitude and tears, had only been able to stammer again, "If—if I were marrying a prince or a duke . . . Oh Dad!"

Now he stayed by her in the pantry, looking at the mushrooms and jingling his keys. "I suppose your Mother wants all that," and he sighed and went away.

There was one thing that Elspeth was determined to do that morning and that was to give Roderick a good brush, leave him clean, fresh and ordered. As soon as she had finished the mushrooms she whistled him up and took him into the cloakroom.

"From the moment you come to St. Faith's," Sister Monica had said, "you will own nothing in the world. Here we don't say 'my cell,' 'my bed'; everything belongs to the Order and is lent to you. Not even the handkerchief you use is yours, you understand?"

"Yes, Sister."

"That isn't hard," said Sister Monica. "It's surprisingly easy. You will see. It will come quite naturally."

That had been true of most things, Elspeth might almost say of everything—except Roderick.

"You will remember his water, Aunt Bevis?"

"I shall remember."

But who will take him for long walks in the woods? Who will understand him? Roderick was not anybody's dog, not like most spaniels; his moods were as dark as his coat; sometimes Elspeth would think there was a being shut up in Roderick, a captured beast, who looked out of his eyes and wrung his heart and made him disagreeable.

"He doesn't mean to be cross. He needs understanding, Aunt Bevis."

"I shall try and understand him."

"When he gets a stick and puts his paw on it, it means he only wants you to pretend to take it; he wants to bounce away with it himself, and when he growls and lies by himself, he's unhappy and then you must leave him and only show you love him very much—and remember he's an actor, Aunt Bevis. When he pretends he doesn't want his food, he wants it very much . . ."

Not even Aunt Bevis could have patience for that! If—if I had known what it was like to leave Roderick, perhaps I shouldn't have gone, thought Elspeth, but that's *disgraceful!* What, mind more about a spaniel than Father, more than Mother or Aunt Bevis! How can I? thought Elspeth, but she could. A dog cannot stand in the way of humans, it is not fitting, but, "He's so innocent, Aunt Bevis." Now, as she brushed him, Elspeth saw that it was dangerous to go near Roderick that morning; she could not trust herself and tears fell on his head and ran, shining, down his black coat, helpless warm tears.

"Elspeth!"

She whipped round. It was Larry Bannerman. Larry arrived early. He was standing in the doorway of the cloakroom, looking at her with an expression on his face that made her turn back quickly to Roderick; even Roderick was safer than that look on Larry's face. Roderick pierced her, but she pierced Larry. Oh, how silly everything is, thought Elspeth.

"Why do you let them make you go?" said Larry. His voice was angry.

"No one's making me go. I want to go," said Elspeth.

"Then why are you crying?" said Larry.

"Don't you expect me to feel it?" said Elspeth angrily too.

They hurled these angry questions at each other.

"Do you think I'm made of stone?" cried Elspeth.

"Yes," said Larry tersely.

Stone! Marble! Hard as nails! Oh, I'm not. I'm not. She began to cry again.

Larry took one step nearer. "Elspeth, Elspeth! My little love!" His voice shook with feeling.

"Larry, *please* go away."

He came nearer. "You don't want to go."

"I do! I do!"

"It's an idea that's got hold of you."

"No, Larry! No!" said Elspeth breathlessly between the pent-up sobs that shook her. "It's—it's my life." She might have said, "Don't you see, I'm fighting for my life."

"Elspeth, I love you." He stood there just above her, his eyes pleading, very much as Roderick's eyes pleaded when they looked up at her, only Larry's looked down. Elspeth did not know herself what it was in her that made her able to harden her heart, even against these two; that gave her strength to do it. "Elspeth."

She whispered, "Larry, couldn't you love Jean?"

His eyes blazed and he said, "You're not the only one who can fix their heart on something." At that Elspeth burst into sobs, crying aloud, "Oh Larry! Go aw-a-ay!" He turned on his heel and went. Elspeth could hear his steps ringing on the tiles of the back passage and she cried helplessly, her sobs stifled against Roderick's coat.

"Elspeth! El-speth! Lady Bannerman is here, and Co-lin."

Let me run away, thought Elspeth. She felt hunted. I shall go now. Say goodbye to Roderick and leave him in the kitchen with Marlowe and get my coat and bag and get on a bus and go there by myself. I can't stand it, thought Elspeth. I can't stand any more.

There were only a few minutes more, not many minutes, an hour or two, before that door in Chiswick would shut on her, before the calm, the peace and sanctity would ring her round and she would be safe, attained, achieved. It was near but it seemed far away with these minutes that lay between, these painful pricking minutes. She shut her eyes and the tears ran out under her lids. I can't stand—all the—pricks.

"Elspeth, your mother's calling you." Elspeth's eyes flew open and her chin went up. It was Larry's voice again but mercifully he did not come in. He spoke from the passage outside and, again, she heard his steps going away. She heard the front door bell ring, Marlowe's steps in the hall; then Aunt Euphrosyne's voice shrilled with Mother's. She heard Uncle Arthur's boom and Roderick struggled to get down. He had a passion for Uncle Arthur. Elspeth put him down on the floor and he tore out. She heard Uncle Arthur's "*Hullo*, little dog!" and Mother's "Get down, Roddy. Down!" and then "Elspeth! Elspeth!"

"Just getting tidy," called Elspeth in a loud voice and began splashing her face with cold water, trying to cool her red eyes. Then she heard Mother's quick pattering steps, her high heels on the passage outside.

"Elspeth, what are you doing in there?"

"I have been brushing Roddy."

"Brushing Roddy! Everyone's here."

"I'm just coming, Mother."

"You know that the men want the cloakroom for wash-ing their hands." Mother sounded cross.

"Yes, Mother."

"Come along. It looks so rude."

Elspeth combed her hair with Father's old comb, rolled down her sleeves; she would have to leave her face and hope no one would notice. "Now for it," said Elspeth and she dug her nails into her palms. She saw Mother's slight tall form in the gray pleated dress at the door of the draw-ing room; "Tchk!" said Mother and bent down to pick a thread off the carpet. Then she went in. Elspeth heard her voice saying, "Of course, the poor child has had a great deal to do." Elspeth flinched but she had to go in. Swiftly, breathlessly, she crossed the hall and in a moment she found herself taking round glasses on a little tray, handing cigarettes in the silver box as she had a hundred times be-fore; this—this is what I have been bred to do, thought Elspeth, but after a little while she saw that everything was different; different in the way their eyes looked at her; the contrast in their voices as they greeted her; they seemed to edge away from her, draw together against her. Am I imagining it? thought Elspeth. Then she found herself talking to Colin Crump.

Colin Crump had always been a joke to them; he had been asked to every party she could remember, usually to make the numbers even or because boys were short. "What happens to him in between?" asked Jean. "Perhaps he only comes to life for parties," said Morna. As long as they could remember, he had been there: first as a little boy with eyes in owlish glasses and sticking-out front teeth, who stammered, then as a large boy with even thicker glasses and a gold plate and a voice that went up and down; and latterly as this young man, Colin Crump, whose stammer was fixed, but whose glasses were thicker than ever. His eyes looked owlish still as they glowed into Elspeth's. She and her cousins had always run away from him, tried to skip his dances, particularly Elspeth; now she could not escape. "I—I think this is splendid of you, El-Elspeth," said Colin Crump confidentially, and Elspeth was startled into looking at him. "I d-don't know how you found the c-courage to st-ick out for your own way . . ." he was saying, "but of c-course you always d-did."

"Did I?" asked Elspeth uncertainly.

"That's what always made me admire you so t-t-tremendously," said Colin.

She had never known that Colin Crump admired her, or that he could do anything as positive as admire. She felt she should say something. "Did you?" or, "How kind of you," but she could not say that. She could only smile; the smile did not feel real, it felt like a faked simper. She thought everyone in the room was watching her; ostensibly they were talking to one another, laughing, but they never took their eyes off her; they were aware of her. How strange that, in all the familiar gathering, Colin Crump, whom she had never thought of except as a joke, should be the only one to understand her. Colin and, perhaps, Aunt Bevis. She began to feel hotly rebellious, as if something were rising in her under all these eyes, these looks, these thoughts that were completely out of sympathy with her. At the least little signal I shall break, thought Elspeth.

She could see through the door, across the hall to the dining room; the table gleamed with its silver, lace, and the colors of the primulas. She thought of the morning's hurry and fuss and she had a sudden vision of the refectory at St.

Faith's, the empty clean room, no curtains, only windows, the table laid out with a bowl and a cup for each Sister, who brought her own fork and knife and spoon and helped herself from a side table. She remembered the quiet eating while a young novice, perhaps herself soon, stood and read aloud. She saw the colors of the flowers under the statue of the Virgin; the flowers came in their seasons for Her, those that grew in the Convent garden, they did not have to match the pudding. That's not fair of me, thought Elspeth, then she cried: but there one isn't interfered with, broken up; there one can remember, be whole, be the whole of yourself because you are allowed to lose yourself. A longing swept over Elspeth; she felt she could not wait.

The guests had fallen into three circles. The young ones were in the window—except Larry, who kept by his mother, tossing down drink after drink. Lady Bannerman was silent but her eyes kept looking from Elspeth to Jean and back to Elspeth. Jean was looking pretty in her new tweed suit. "Is it tomato color?" asked Elspeth.

"They call it spring red," said Jean.

"It's bright tomato," said Elspeth derisively and then remembered Sister Monica and said, "It suits you." Jean did not hear her. All of them were listening to their elders.

The men were by the fire, talking jerkily. "That damned bullfinch," said Father.

"There's a spring trap on the market now," said Uncle Arthur.

"Herring nets," that was Major Fitzgerald. "They will have every plum if you don't stop 'em; darned little robbers," and they began to talk about apples—a glut of cider apples—and of Major Fitzgerald's Worcester Permains. That was harmless but on the sofa there was the sound of whispers. In spite of the forbidding silence of Larry and his mother, the women were on the topic of Elspeth. It was

Aunt Euphrosyne who whispered. Mrs. Baldock leaned forward to hear; her blue straw with the white bow met Aunt Euphrosyne's feathers; Mother's head was in between. "Utterly, utterly selfish," Elspeth heard; and Jean heard and Morna and Larry and Colin Crump, the whole room, and Elspeth felt a burning color flood her neck.

"Ribston Pippins," said Father loudly.

"Can't beat 'em," said Major Fitzgerald.

After all it was Aunt Bevis who precipitated it. Aunt Bevis had been sitting with an expression on her face that showed, Elspeth thought, that she was worrying over the food. She had argued with Mother that there was not enough chicken; "We should have had three from the farm, not two," said Aunt Bevis; now, suddenly, she spoke; perhaps if she had not been worrying over the chickens she would not have spoken as bluntly. "How dare you badger the child," said Aunt Bevis. "Yes, how dare you!" Elspeth began to tremble and Colin turned. To her horror Colin joined in. "You—you shouldn't," said Colin Crump, stuttering and swallowing. "D-do you remember," he said and the words seemed to swell with the difficulty he had to get them out—as words are difficult for me, thought Elspeth, wishing he would be silent, but he was determined to go on. "Do you re-member, Mrs. Ersk-kine, when they c-came to C-Christ and said His mother and His brethren were st-standing without . . . ?" He could not go on, he was as scarlet as Elspeth, but, "Yes," said Aunt Bevis furiously and loudly. "Do you remember what Christ said?"

"I remember, Bevis," said Mother, her voice high. "I remember and I have always thought it was heartless. Heartless!"

There was such a silence that if Roderick had shed one hair on the carpet it would have been heard. Every eye in the room, whether it looked at her or not, was turned on Elspeth. She had never felt as exposed. Sister Monica had told her not to speak but now it was as if, willy nilly, through Colin and Aunt Bevis she had spoken, as if she had been given a voice. Then justify it, thought Elspeth in agony.

St. Elizabeth found her apron full of roses. St. Teresa had levitation. The wind changed for St. Joan. "Oh God!" prayed Elspeth, her lips silent, her hands sticky.

If, through the open window, a wind had swept in and filled all the room with sound; if she, Elspeth, could have been lifted up, even two feet from the carpet, lifted without a hand touching her; if roses had fallen or their scent perfumed the room, even one or two roses, but she was left. There was no help, no vindication.

She had to stand there before them all, helpless and silent. She could feel her heart beating hurtfully; for a moment she could only feel the hurt, the smart, and then it became a tiny echo, echoing down two thousand years—no, nineteen hundred and sixty, thought Elspeth. The drawing room seemed to swim round her and she heard Reverend Mother Dorothea's words; those near voices faded and Mother Dorothea's, calm, authoritative, directed her, "No fireworks."

Elspeth's hands unclenched and, as if she had broken the tension, everyone relaxed. The clock ticked, Uncle Arthur cleared his throat, Roderick stretched and sighed blissfully at Uncle Arthur's feet; Mother gave a quick little sob and dabbed her eyes. Everywhere conversation broke out.

"Ribston Pippins? Yes, nothing to beat them," said Mr. Baldock.

"They had a nice brown corduroy skirt with a little checked coat, but I chose this," said Jean.

"Have you heard the S-Simmons are having a band for their d-dance?" asked Colin Crump of Morna.

"From the Crane Club. It will cost a fortune; quite ridiculous!" called Aunt Euphrosyne.

Lady Bannerman passed her drink to Larry. Larry drank it.

"Bevis, it's a quarter past. Don't you think . . . ?" said Mother, but just then Marlowe sounded the gong.

# *Flowering Dagger*

## ROSEMARY SUTCLIFF

Below the Royal Village the stream broke up into a chain of alder-fringed pools; and it was there, just about the cattle ford, that the women brought their washing. Soon it would be a place of thick shadows, and sunspots dancing through the alder leaves to freckle the dark water, and maybe a hovering dragonfly to light the shadows. That was still to come; all the good days of summer still to come. Now the leaves were only a green smoke, too thin to keep out the young sunshine, and the cuckoo calling across the valley was a new and shining sound.

Saba, the High Chief's younger daughter cocked her head to it in delight, calling back softly, "Cuck-oo—Cuck-oo." And her heart lifted to the wide green springtime smell of the world after the enclosed smoky darkness of the house place through the winter moons.

"Cuck-oo! Cuck-oo!" It was only the fourteenth spring that she had greeted.

She pulled her brother Garim's best tunic from the pile beside her, and plunged it into the shallows, then flung it wide over the bank, heavy with water, its blue and brown checker darkened almost to black, and began to pound and squeeze it this way and that, beating it with the small round stone in the hollow of her hand.

Close beside her, Cordaella her sister was scrubbing an old but still serviceable kilt of her man's, and smiling at it as she scrubbed. Cordaella had been married all but a moon now, to Maelgun Swift-Spear, chosen for her by their father and the Priest Kind because he was strong among the young warriors, and of the right degree of kinship to mate with the Royal Daughter of the Tribe. Cordaella seemed to like him well enough, and these days she had the bloom on her, the warm secret look that Saba had seen before in girls who had been making the man-and-woman magic, and found it good. Nevertheless, glancing aside at her, Saba was glad that she was only the younger daughter, and within limits and the custom of the Tribe, might choose and be chosen for herself, when the time came.

The girls and women laughed and chattered together as they worked. Someone began to sing, softly, for herself and anyone else who cared to listen; a man-child clad in a coral bead on a thong round his fat little middle, too young to be left at home, too young to swim, walked into the pool and was pulled out and soundly slapped by his mother, and for a while after drowned all other sounds with his bull-calf bellowings.

Presently, when the shadows of the alder branches had moved over toward evening on the clean washing that was now spread to dry along the bank, a knot of young men came down the green track that dipped to the ford. Hunters returned from a day's hunting, two of them carrying the spear-slung carcass of a roe doe, their hounds padding at their heels. They splashed across the ford, the hounds checking to shake themselves on the near bank, and went on up the track towards the village. All save one of the hounds. A young brindled bitch, full of the friendliest intentions, had broken away from the rest, and was heading straight up the streamside toward where the women were gathered. Two of the hunting party came after her, since it seemed that whistling was no use; but by the time Garim, the foremost in pursuit, had caught up with her and hauled her off, by a hand twisted in her rawhide collar, more than one of the drying garments bore the wet and woodland traces of hound's paws and human feet.

Amid the protests of the other women, Cordaella snatched up an armful of the nearest, glaring. "Garim! Can you not master your own hounds? All these will have to be washed again!"

No man likes the suggestion that he cannot control his own dog, especially if it be true. Garim flushed crimson. "Kea is little more than a puppy. She meant no harm. If your washing ground is sacred, you should plant a fence of spears round it!"

Cordaella stood confronting him, the spoiled washing clutched to her breast, and about her an air of high tragedy. "With such heedless fools as you running loose, it is in my mind that we should indeed! It is not even your own cloak that you have fouled! But you have always thought that because you are the High Chief's son—"

Garim, his hand still through the collar of the young bitch, stood leaning on his spear, and watched his raging sister with an air of detached interest. "I will tell you a thing, Royal Daughter," he said, when she seemed to have finished, "there are times when you grow shrill as a shrew mouse."

"Oh! You—you—" Cordaella threw the washing at him.

Saba was scarcely aware of them. All her sudden awareness had gone to the tall boy standing a little behind Garim, and seemingly as remote from the quarrel as she. Brychan, one of the hostages in her father's Hall.

In the old days there had been a constant ragged warfare of the slave and cattle-raiding along the borders between her people and the people farther toward the Sunrise. It had been on one such raid that old Marrag, who was young then, had been captured, old Marrag who had been her own nurse and Cordaella's and their mother's before them. There was peace between the two Tribes now; but a somewhat fragile peace; and to give it strength, every seven years there was an exchange of hostages, three young warriors sent by each Tribe to spend their next seven years among the young warriors of the other. They were treated as equals in every way; sometimes friendships were formed, and brotherhoods sworn that lasted for life. But nonetheless they were hostages, and if their own Tribe broke the peace, their lives would be the first to pay for it. Brychan had been with Saba's Tribe for more than a year, and she had seen him often among the New Spears, the young warriors. She had even poured the barley beer for him in her father's Hall when the women went round with the narrow-necked drink jars. But she had never really looked at him before. With his mane of mouse-fair hair, his bony freckled face, and thin shoulders that had not yet broadened into a man's, there had not seemed anything special to look at. But she was looking now, a little puzzled by her own looking. And a breath of wind was flickering the alder leaves, and the cuckoo was still calling from somewhere across the valley; and Brychan was looking at her, as though that too was for the first time.

Suddenly, joyously, and in the same instant, they smiled at each other, as though in first greeting, as though they had known each other all their lives.

The quarrel, it seemed, was over. The quarrels between Garim and Cordaella generally ended as quickly as they began. And Garim, the hound bitch at his heel, was on his way up the bank, calling over his shoulder to Brychan, "Hai! Come then, or they will be claiming our share of the kill!"

Brychan turned and went after him, and Saba joined Cordaella and the rest in gathering up the scattered washing. The muddied garments that must be washed again would have to wait till tomorrow. Too late in the day to start again now.

She thought no more of Brychan through the rest of that day. But at night, lying on the fern-piled bed place in the little hut in the Women's Quarters, that she had to herself now that Cordaella was married, suddenly in the drifting moment between waking and sleeping, she saw him again. Saw everything about him; things she had not been aware of seeing at all, among the streamside alders. Not just his face, the shape of his eyes set level under thick fair brows, the mouth that seemed too wide for his bony jawline, the freckles that gave him a boy's look still, but everything, the way he stood, the way he held his spear; even the white scar, narrow as a leaf vein, on the brown of his spear hand, just above the thumb. Still on the edge of sleep, she wondered what it would be like to be touched by him. And the thought startled her awake, because it was so new and strange. She lay sharply wakeful for a while after that, filled with an odd excitement and a sense of waiting, she did not know for what, and listening to the quiet breathing of Den, the little slave her father had given her, who slept across the doorway. Den was not like old Nurse, captured in war, she was one of the little Dark People, here before the coming of the Tribe who were now their lords and masters. They were not quite of the daylight, the Dark People, they Knew Things. If ever she had a secret to keep, she thought, she must be careful of Den. And that too, was a strange new thought . . . But sleep took her at last; and when she woke in the morning the strangeness had fallen away behind her on the other side of sleep, and the world had returned, almost, to its everyday self.

In the days that followed, she saw Brychan from time to time, just as she had done before. But the magic seemed to have passed with the moment, swift as the blue flash of a diving kingfisher. Perhaps also there was in both of them a sense of warning against trying to catch it back. Among Saba's people, it was forbidden to mate outside the Tribe. No good could come of looking each other's way again, though the wind still flickered the alder leaves, and the cuckoo called from across the valley.

And then the cuckoo changed his note, and it was the eve of Midsummer. And at sunrise the girls were off and away, along the streamside and up the wooded combes of the High Chalk, seeking flowers to braid with the magic vervain into their hair, for the dancing that would come at nightfall with the waking of the Fire.

Saba soon left the group of girls with whom she had set out, and drifted off by herself, making for a place she knew of, a sheltered tangle of hazel and elder and wayfaring trees, where the dark blue dove flowers grew. She found and gathered three stalks of the winged blossoms, with a small thrill of delight, because this was the first Midsummer that she had been old enough to garland her hair and dance among the women's side. Then she went searching elsewhere. Lower down, the thickets were starred with wild white roses, but she knew that those, gathered in the morning, would be limp and sad as dead moths by dusk, and left them to their growing. She found a strand of early honeysuckle, creamy clover heads, scabious and freckled orchis of the open Chalk; and pulled the breen linen web from her hair to carry them in; they would travel better so. In a patch of low-growing scrub murmurous with bees, she checked to break off a milky curd of elder blossom. She did not need it; she had more than enough flowers for three garlands already; she gathered it simply for the prodigal joy of gathering; and still carrying it in her hand, stepped out onto the faint sheep track that skirted the thicket—and came face to face with Brychan following it up from the farther valley.

Startled, she said the first and most obvious thing that came into her head. "Brychan! There's no hunting in these runs; what brings you up here into shepherd country?"

"I might knock over a hare." He checked, leaning on his spear. "No, I have been over to Gray Stones to ask Drustic to sell me one of Fleetfoot's pups. But I have left it too late, they are all spoken for."

"I am sorry."

He shrugged. "There will be other pups."

"I have been flower hunting, for my Midsummer garland," Saba said a little breathlessly; as though, having demanded what brought him there, she owed him a like explanation.

He said suddenly and softly, "And so we are come to the same place at the same time."

She was not sure whether he was laughing at her or not, and so left him unanswered, while, with exaggerated care, she added the scented curd of elder blossom she still carried to the rest of her gathering. The next thing happened very suddenly. An amber-furred bee had settled among the flowers without her noticing it and, disturbed by their rearrangement, blundered up into her face. Instinctively she made to brush it aside and, as she did so, felt a small fiery dart of pain below her right eye.

She dropped her flowers with a little cry: "A bee! It has stung me—"

"Let me look," the boy said. He laid down his spear and, taking her by the shoulders, turned her to the sunlight. The small fiery pain was spreading along her cheek.

"That is a bad place for a sting! And the barb still there. Wait now, I will get it out for you and there will be small harm done."

He pulled a little dagger from his belt, and tipped her face, with his fingers under her chin. "Look up. So—now hold still, I will not hurt you."

"I do not mind if you hurt me," Saba said, faintly scornful. "Only get it out. I am not wishing to look as if I had been in an ale fight before the dancing starts."

She felt a small prick; a bright clear fleck of pain, white amid the red of the bee burning. And then the burning ceased to spread, seemed to grow less.

"Is it out?"

"It is out. Soon the smarting will ease. Look—"

He held the tiny black sting out to her on the point of his dagger. His fingers were no longer under her chin, but she seemed still to feel them there, more vividly, more frighteningly, with more of delight than she had ever felt anything before. She knew now what it was like to be touched by him. She looked at the sting, then at the dagger in his hand. It seemed better not to look at Brychan himself, not just now. "Show me."

"I am showing you."

"No, not the sting, your dagger. I have not seen its like before."

He flicked off the sting, and held the dagger out to her. "Take it, and look." And something in the way he did so told her that it was a treasure, and that it was not everyone he would let handle it. She took it from him in the same way, and stood turning it over. It was a small dagger, but deadly; sharp as the bee's sting. Nothing special about the hilt, except that it was of a kind she did not know. It was the blade that held the magic. A blade of the rare and precious metal that men called iron, inlaid with three silver flowers, the largest just below the hilt, each one below it growing smaller with the taper of the blade. They too were of a kind that she did not know; a little like bell flowers, but not quite; more like the slender green-and-white star lilies she had found sometimes in the woods. Beautiful.

"What are the flowers?" she asked.

"I do not know. The dagger came from far away. Maybe the flowers are from far away too."

"It is beautiful," she said, and gave it back into the hand he held out for it.

"It is the only thing that is truly mine," he said. And then quickly, as though afraid she might ask more, "Does the smarting grow less?"

"It is almost gone."

"Still, you should go home, and put some cooling thing on it."

But they stood motionless, knowing, both of them, that she should gather up her scattered flowers and he his spear, and they should be on their way. Saba brought up her eyes at last to his face, and they stood and looked at each other Then they did an odd thing, in the same instant they each put up a hand to the other, and fitted them together; not holding, just touching, palm to palm, fingertips to fingertips, like the two halves of something that had been parted coming lightly and surely together. "I must go," she said. It seemed to her that something, some living part of herself, was flowing out to him through their touching hands, some part of him flowing in to her.

"I must go," she said again, desperately.

"And get that sting place salved." For an instant his thumb moved outward and curled round hers. Then they parted hands.

"My old nurse is wise in the way of herbs." Saba knelt and gathered up her fallen flowers, gently shaking off the dying bee that lay among them. She wished that she had not brushed it away. If she had stood quite still, it might have worked the sting out for itself and flown off unharmed. She did not want anything in the world to be hurt or dying. Yesterday, that would have seemed a foolish thought; but yesterday was gone . . .

"I wish I had not killed it," she said.

Now that Old Nurse was growing old indeed, and had the pains in her joints that often came to old people, she had a small living hut of her own on the edge of the village. Saba had once asked her if she never wanted to go back to her own people. But she had said, "What would I be wanting that for? It is all so long ago. There would be no one left who remembers me. Here, I have the children that I have reared, and the world that I have grown used to. I do well enough where I am."

And certainly she looked contented enough that morning, squatting on her painted stool outside the door hole of her little turf-roofed bothie, nodding over a torn cloak that she was patching, while her big half-wild cat dozed on the edge of the turf roof just over her head, blinking amber eyes in the sunlight.

She roused at Saba's coming, and looked sideways up at her. "You have been gathering your Midsummer garland? Well then, let you show me."

Saba opened her bundle to show. "There was a bee with the flowers. It stung me here—under my eye."

"Aiee! That is a bad place to be stung!" said old Marrag, much as Brychan had done. "Let me look." She got up, letting the patched cloak fall in a tangle to her feet; and also as Brychan had done, put her hand under the girl's chin, turning her face to the light. The sour smell of old flesh came from her; but all at once Saba saw that she had been beautiful when she was young—under the sagging and withered skin, her bones were beautiful still.

"You are flushed, and your eyes are very bright," the old woman said. "Little bird, have you a fever?"

"No, it is only the sting, and that I have come running."

"Well, the sting is cleanly out."

"Brychan got it out for me."

"Brychan?"

"One of the hostages."

"And what were you doing, up and away with one of the hostages?"

"Nothing. A bee stung me, and he came by, and got it out with his dagger. He did it so carefully that I scarcely felt it." But she had felt other things, his touch on her face, the strange current that had been like life itself passing between them through their joined palms. Suddenly her heart began to race; and once again there was the sense of warning in her; and she followed Marrag into the warm shadows of the bothie, she began to babble of the thing that could not matter, to cover the deeper silence over the things that did. "It is the most beautiful dagger I have ever seen—not like ours at all—an iron blade, it has; so small, but sharp, and beautiful—and silver flowers on the blade—"

Old Nurse, reaching up for a little jar among several standing on the crossbeam, started violently and knocked it over. "Tch! Tch! I grow clumsy in my old age," she scolded; and then stooped groaningly to gather up the small wreckage. "Silver flowers on the blade? A strange kind of dagger that sounds to be."

"It is not like any dagger that ever I saw before." Saba knelt to help her. "He said it came from very far away."

"And what are they like, these flowers?"

"A little like star lilies. Three of them—just a silver pattern inlaid into the blade." Saba began to wish that she had not mentioned the dagger either. But it seemed that Old Nurse had lost interest. She was reaching down some more salve.

"Now, turn your face to the door. There, is that not cool and soothing? Now there will be no swelling, and all the finest of the New Spears will be wanting you to leap with them through the embers, when the Fire dies down tonight on the Dancing Hill."

And then in the last moment, she took Saba's face between her old twisted hands, and stood looking down into it—she was a tall old woman still—as though she was looking for the answer to a question. "But let you have no more to do with this Brychan. I have seen—I have heard of such daggers before. They do indeed come from far off, and are not of mortal making; and those who carry them must serve them; and bring black sorrow upon all who come too near."

For the moment a little shadow seemed to fall across the shine of Saba's morning. But she left it behind her with the crowding shadows in the bothie. "Old Nurse is trying to frighten me. Maybe she is jealous because I have been all hers. Or maybe she thinks I am still too young to—" She left the thought unfinished. It seemed better not to finish it. Not just yet . . .

She began to run, the flower-filled net swinging in her

hand, down toward the stream, where the other girls would be already making their garlands.

At dusk, throughout the Royal Village, throughout all the villages of the Tribe, the fires were quenched on every hearth. And with the dying of the last fire, the Festival of Midsummer was begun, and it was time to raise the New Fire, the Need Fire, the Living Fire that must be born afresh each year.

Then a strangeness came over the world, as it came every year between the fires. And in silence, and something that had in it both expectancy and fear, the people wound their way up the steep shoulder of the downs above the village, past the ancient strong place that could hold the whole Clan in time of danger, to the Dancing Hill beyond. They thronged the level hill crest, crowding shadows brushed with the light of a lopsided honeysuckle moon. No sound among them save the soughing of a little wind through the thorn scrub. And in their midst the dark fire stack waiting, as the whole night waited, for the wonder of the reborn fire. The first team of warriors took up the trailing rawhide ropes of the fire drill, and began the swift rhythmic pull and release, pull and release, the long step forward and the long swing back that set the sharp-nosed spindle whirling in its socket. Team followed team, one taking over as another tired, while the moon rose higher and whiter; and the people waited, watching, half-fearful as they were half-fearful every year, that this year the wonder would not come.

But at last it came. A smell of charring, a thread of smoke fronding up into the moonlight, a single spark that fell on the dried moss, to be followed by another, and another, a licking yellow petal of flame. A soft long breath of relief and exultation broke from the crowd, as Cuthlin,

Chief of the Oak Priests, bent and caught the flame on his torch of plaited straw, and whirled it into a blaze, a spinning sun wheel of light, then turned to the darkly waiting fire stack.

Fire was born again, the life of the Tribe was born again for another year. And as the threads of brightness spread through the brushwood, and the bigger branches caught and crackled into ragged tongues of flame, and the light reached out to leap and flutter on the faces of those nearest among the crowd, Saba looked for Brychan, and could not find him. Maybe he was there, somewhere farther back in the throng, in the moon-brushed dark where the firelight could not reach. Maybe he had not troubled to come up from the village. This was not his Tribe, not his Need Fire on the Hill of Dancing. And so he would not see her with her Midsummer garland round her head, and she need not have taken such trouble with it after all.

Later, when the chanting was done, and the dancing over, the long snaking sun dance, and the young warriors whirling and stamping to the rhythm of the wolfskin drums; when the flames that had leapt skyward, casting their fierce and fitful glare all across the Dancing Hill, were sinking low, the warriors and their women who wished for sons in the coming year linked hands and leaped through the sinking fire. And then the young warriors who had no wives of their own as yet began to catch the girls of their choice out of the women's side, to leap with them.

Govan, whom she had always thought among the fairest and fiercest of the young warriors, came and tried to catch Saba's hand, but she thrust him off, and he shrugged and went elsewhere. She could have had her choice of three, that night, the first night that ever she had worn the magic vervain in her hair. But she wanted none of them.

And now, before the flames sank too low, it was time to be taking the New Fire, the Need Fire, to quicken the hearths of the Clan for another year. And the youngest men of each household began to come forward, those who lived in the Royal Village merely dipping a branch in the flames, and running, with it streaming out in smoking mares' tails behind them, while those whose homes were the outlands farms, and the shepherd's and herdsman's bothies among the folds of the High Chalk, took carefully chosen embers and stowed them in fire pots. Now, men were stamping out the last dragon-red gleeds on the blackened fire scars; and all around, the crowd was crumbling away, melting into the moony night that would soon turn toward morning.

A hand closed on Saba's, drawing her backward into the anonymous darkness. She did not start, or even look round to see who it was. She turned and ran with Brychan down the hill slope away from the village.

In the midst of a little hollow filled with elder and wayfaring trees, they flung themselves down, arms round each other, breathless and half-laughing, straining close.

"I wanted to jump through the fire with you," Brychan said, muffled, into the hollow of her neck. He was pulling off her Midsummer garland, and her hair tumbled loose across them both.

"I wanted it too." It was strange, they had never even touched before this morning. Now they were so much a part of each other that there was nothing she could not say to him, nothing that must be held back. "Oh, I wanted it till the want ached in my belly."

"Was that why you pushed Govan away?"

"I could not," she said, "I could not bear Govan's sons!" And then she heard what she had said, and a great stillness took them both. No sound but the little night wind hushing through the elder branches. The white curds of blossom swayed in the dark leaf mass above them, and a shower of moon flecks scattered through. "I did not say that," Saba said. "If I did, I have forgotten."

"You did say it, and you have not forgotten." Brychan's arms tightened round her.

"You are holding me too hard—I cannot breathe—"

"And it is forbidden to marry outside the Tribe. Oh, I know that." But he did not loose his hold.

"It is against the Law, and the Custom which is stronger than the Law. We are too far apart . . ." How smooth and cool the skin of his back was; just the faint raised lines of the warrior tattooing across his shoulders.

"I will think of a way," he said. "There must *be* a way. Saba, listen, the gods wouldn't make us feel like this together, as though—as though we were part of each other, if we weren't—if there wasn't a way to find—"

He was half on top of her. He began to kiss her; hard, inexpert kisses that pushed her lips against her teeth until she opened them to him. His mouth was warm in hers, much warmer than the skin of his back. Little ripples of sensation began to run through her, a stranger shimmering that rose and rose in her body as though in answer to something, and was like nothing that she had ever known before. She must strain against him, closer and closer, until they blended together and became the same thing. One hand was round the back of his neck now; she felt the dry springy strength of his hair between her fingers—and something else.

"There's a thing on the back of your neck—I'll get it off—" She dug in a sharp thumbnail.

He yelped, and twisted away from her. "Wah! That's me!"

"It is a leech—"

"It's not, it's a bit of me. I was born with it!" He rubbed
the back of his neck. "You have drawn blood, little she-
cat!"

They began to laugh, lying loose to each other now, and
the moment passed and went leaf-light down the wind.
The green plover were calling over the Chalk. Brychan sat
up, then scrambled to his feet, reaching to pull her up after
him. "Soon the light will be coming. It is time that you
were back in your father's Hall."

On the day after the Midsummer Fires, the High Chieftain rode out as he did every year, to circle the boundaries
of the Tribal Lands; his hearth companions and certain of
the young warriors with him. And among them, this year,
rode Brychan.

They were gone close on half a moon, for it was a matter of feasting at the hearth of every lesser chieftain; the
exchange of gifts; long sittings beside Council Fires. And
for Saba, left behind in the Royal Village, the waiting days
were strange ones, following a surface pattern of activity
that was like the pattern of all the familiar days that had
gone before. And beneath the familiar surface, not like any
day that she had ever known. Empty, for lack of Brychan,
yet full of him because he was in everything; in the way
the light fell through a leaf, in the sound of rain dripping
from the thatch, in the taste of barley bannock, in the
crimson wool that she was weaving on the loom—all color
seemed more brilliant in those days—in the softness of her
own skin when she touched it where his hands had been.
She was aware of all things, of life itself, as she had been
when she was a child; only when you were a child, she
thought, you did not know you had the mystery, and
when you grew older and lost the shining awareness, you
forgot . . . She felt very close to the heart of things; and

very kind. She had a great sense of kindness toward all life in those waiting days, and surely the kindness of all life toward herself in return. And soon Brychan would be back. She did not look beyond the moment of his coming. Something deep within her turned her away from that. Enough to hold the shining, fragile happiness in her cupped hands, and know that in a little while he would come back.

And then one evening, the High Chieftain and his following rode home. And next morning, with the summer mist scarfing the course of the stream, and the shining midge clouds already dancing in the clear air above it, Saba went down with the other girls as usual to fetch water from the stream, and made an excuse to linger behind. Brychan, who knew the pattern of the village's day, would guess where to find her.

Now they sat together between the roots of an ancient willow tree that spread its shelter down the bank.

"Have you missed me?" they had asked and answered, for the joy of asking and answering: and "Do you love me still?" They had kissed. And now the future that Saba had been so careful not to look at too closely was upon them.

"You said you would think of a way," Saba told him, her face against his shoulder. "You said the gods would not make us feel like this, if there wasn't a way."

"I know. But it's hard to find."

"If we were to go away together, and build our hearth far, far off, where no one knew the name of my father's Tribe—where there were no people at all—"

"I am a hostage," Brychan said heavily. "If we did that, there would be black trouble between your Tribe and mine."

A willow wren was singing somewhere in the low-hanging branches.

"In five years, you will not be a hostage. I would wait

five years. I would wait all my life, if I might be with you in the end."

"Even if they tried to make you go to Govan or another among your father's warriors?"

"Yes," said Saba.

And the willow wren sang on. And in a little, she added, almost weeping, "But in five years, I shall still be of my Tribe, and you of yours."

Brychan put his arms round her and began with clumsy gentleness to rock her to and fro. Over the top of her head he was staring out along the valley. His face, when she looked up at him, was very white, unless that was the morning mist and the green shade of the willow leaves; and there was a deep-cut frown line between his thick fair brows. "As to that—" he began at last, and checked.

She made a small questioning sound.

"As to that—" Suddenly he seemed to make up his mind, and the words came out in an almost painful rush. "I've thought and thought, all these days and nights, until my head and my heart are sore with thinking, but—Saba, I was not born in the Women's Place behind my father's—my foster father's Hall. I was found lying on his threshold, none knowing how I came there. And beside me, my dagger with the silver flowers. Did I not tell you it was the only thing that was truly my own? He reared me as a son at his hearth; but when the time came for exchanging hostages—he sent me in place of his own. I swore silence, with my hands on his thigh, and now I am an oathbreaker for your sake, Saba—Saba—"

She ignored that part of it, leaping with sudden unreasoning hope to the implication of his story. "So you are likely not of—of your own Tribe at all, and if not that, you might even be of mine."

"What use if I was?" Brychan said in a small miserable

burst of fury. "We could not stand in the daylight and claim it. I have broken my oath to no purpose."

But even then, he did not try to bind the oath silence upon her. And she was glad of that; that he should know there was no need. "We should know in our own hearts," she said, clinging to him. "In five summers' time—we should know . . . I must go back, or they will miss me in the women's quarters."

And she tore herself free, and scrambled to her feet and ran.

But still with her was the feeling that because she wanted to be kind to all life, life must want to be kind to her. And as she ran, she was remembering something that she had not thought of since the eve of Midsummer. She had had no reason to remember it. Now, suddenly, all that was changed. She did not go to join the other women, but to Marrag's bothie. Old Marrag was sitting on her painted stool beside the hearth, for the early sunshine was still thin for old bones outside; and she went and squatted beside her, with her hair shaken forward so that her face was shadowed.

"So you come again. You have not been, these past days," the old woman said.

And that was true. Old Nurse saw too much, and Saba had too much to hide.

"Old Nurse, when I came to you with a bee sting for salving, at Midsummer, and told you that Brychan had got out the barb—and about his dagger, why did you start, and knock over the pot of salve— You are very wise. Do you know something that other people do not know?" She was holding the old woman's knees, and she felt them grow rigid.

"What should I know, Little Bird?"

"Something about that dagger with the silver flowers?"

The old woman jerked forward and, thrusting back the heavy curtain of hair, peered deep into the girl's face. Then, at what she saw there, gave a low moaning cry. "Aiee! Fool and worse than fool that I was! But I thought you still a child. Too young—too young . . ."

"The dagger, Old Nurse."

"I will tell you. I will tell. But first, let you tell me—have you made the man-and-woman magic with this Brychan?"

Saba shook her head. "Almost, after the Midsummer Fire was sunk." Laughter ached in her throat. "But he has a mole on the back of his neck, and I thought it was a leech and tried to pull it off; and he cried out that I had drawn blood—"

"The Great Mother be thanked for that at least. But—a mole on his neck, you say? That too?"

"Have I not said?" Saba gripped Old Nurse's knees and began to shake them. "Tell me! You *shall* tell me!"

Marrag was rocking to and fro like someone hunched over an intolerable pain. A little whimpering moan broke from her. "It is so long ago. So long—and your mother not yet wed. The harvest failed three years running, and the cattle dropped their young untimely; and so there was famine in the land. Then the Priest Kind said the gods were angry, and Lugh of the Shining Spear had turned his face from us, and it was time for the Royal Daughter to hang up her girdle for a sacrifice. So the thing was done, according to the ancient Custom, and a branch-woven bothie made for her beside where the trade road crosses the frontier ford from the South; and her crimson girdle hung from the branch of an alder tree for a sign. And she was left there for the first man who came that way."

Her voice trailed into silence. And after a few moments Saba asked in a small dry whisper, "Who came?"

"A merchant from lands across the great Water—far and

far and far to the South. And when he had played his part, and moved on in the morning, he left her his dagger with silver starlilies on the blade. She showed it to me. I was the only one, I think, she ever showed it to. A strange morning gift, but it was his own and, he had told her, more beautiful than anything in his merchant bales. I have thought, whiles and whiles, that there might have been love between those two, given time for flowering and fruiting . . . He left her something else, too. It was not long before we knew it, she and I, that she was carrying a child. Then there was great rejoicing, for all men know that the birth of such a child is a sign of favor from the gods. 'Lugh's face shines upon us once again!' they said. But your mother did not rejoice, knowing that when it was born, the Priest Kind would take and pour out its blood to quicken the furrows, according to the Custom."

A great stillness, and a great cold was creeping over Saba.

"The child was born, as such children must be, in a hut made sacred, away from all others—only myself with her—a fine man-child with no mark on him save a rose mole on the back of his neck."

The cold reached Saba's heart and tightened round it. "But the Priest Kind took him and shed his life into the furrows."

"It was not him that I showed to the priests, but another, born dead—at least, I suppose it was born dead. There are always children being born among the slave girls and the Dark People, and no one troubles greatly what becomes of them."

"And then?" Saba whispered. Even her lips felt stiff with cold.

"We had nine days. A woman who bears a dead child is Taboo for nine days in the birth hut, only one woman staying to tend her, who is Taboo also. That you know. So I took the babe, as she bade me, and the dagger—his father's dagger—and a skin of milk. And that night I stole away."

"But she was alone."

"Aye, alone. I left her the herbs that she must use. The food that was laid before the threshold she had to fetch for herself when none was by. And I set out for the runs of my own people. I came back to my own village like a beggarwoman, keeping my cloak over my face, lest any should know me again. And I came away under the wing of the dark, leaving the babe behind me, lying on the Chieftain's threshold, and the dagger beside him. And truly I did not think that he would live, taken at birth from his mother, and carried for days through the wild, and not thriving on the ewe milk . . . But I could not wait; I had to be back with your mother before the nine days were up . . ." She was still rocking herself to and fro, to and fro. It was as though if she stopped, she must stop also in the thing that she was forcing herself to tell. "Always, I counted him for dead, though I never told *her* so. And even when you came, with this story of Brychan, and a dagger with three silver flowers on the blade, I thought, 'He will have died, and they will not have let a beautiful dagger the like of that one go to waste.' And I thought, 'They will never have sent a hostage who is not the Chief's true son; they will not have dared!' And I thought, 'She is too young; no harm will come of it.' Aiee. Ochone! Ochone!"

There was a long silence. And then Saba said in that same dreadful little frozen whisper, "And so we are sib to each other, Brychan and I."

"You have the same mother."

"It is true, isn't it? You would not tell me if it was not true?"

"It is true. Why should I tell you a lie that—if you tell it again, I shall die an ugly death. I who am old and wish to die gently beside my own hearth; and the Priest Kind will take Brychan and do with him as they would have done seventeen summers ago; and there will be blood flow again between your Tribe and mine. Why should I tell you what could let all this loose, if it were not that it is true and that I—must tell. Now I have told, and you must never look toward Brychan again."

She must never look toward Brychan again; nor Brychan toward her.

Saba crept out from Old Nurse's bothie like a little gray ghost; and managed to gain her own sleeping hut unseen.

Den was squatting just within the entrance hole, waiting for her. And when she sat down on the edge of the bed place, the little slave crept to her, long dark eyes fixed on her face. "What is it? Let you tell Den."

"I have eaten bad berries, and there is a sickness in my belly," Saba said.

"I will go to Old Marrag."

"I have been to her, and she has given me a thing to drink. Leave me alone, Den. Bide in the doorway, and see that nobody comes near."

All day she sat on the side of the bedplace, her knees drawn up to her chin, staring before her. Once, she heard Cordaella's voice outside, and Den's. But what they said, she did not know. And then Cordaella went away again.

When the dusk deepened beyond the door hole, and the sounds from her father's Hall told her that the evening meal was over, and the breaking up and shifting that always followed it would have begun, she sent the child to find Brychan, and bid him come to her behind the stable sheds. Better to send the child than go seeking him herself; the little Dark People made good messengers, for they could come and go like a draft through a wall chink.

And when Den was gone, she gathered herself together and went out into the dusk, to the appointed meeting place. He was there almost as soon as she was, and would have caught her close; but she pushed him away.

"What is it? The child said you wanted me, and now you will not let me hold you."

She gave him his answer in a broken rush, "Do you mind, on the night of the New Fires, I said we were too far apart? The gods must have laughed, if they were listening. We are too close. We are sib to each other, you and I."

"Sib? You have been sleeping in the moonlight and talk madness!"

"There's no moon." Standing with her hands on his breast to hold him off, she told him all there was to tell.

He heard her out in silence; only she felt him begin to shiver under her hands, as though the night had turned cold. And when she finished, he said in the voice of one trying not to retch, "I wish that old woman had died on her journey, or that my mother—our mother—had borne a dead child indeed."

"I wish that she had borne two," Saba said. And then, "What will we do, Brychan? What will we do?" knowing the answer even while she asked it.

This was a thing they could never escape. No waiting five years, no going away together. It would go with them. It was within them.

Brychan wiped the back of his hand across his mouth. "There is only one way that we can be together," he said, after a long silence; answering her unspoken thought.

She reached out in the dark and felt for the little dagger in his belt. It was cool to her fingers. "This?"

"Yes."

"Do it now," she whispered. "Let us hold very close together, and do it now."

"Not now. We must wait through tonight, to be quite sure."

"I am sure now. I am afraid. But I am sure."

"If you are still sure in the morning, come down to the willow above the ford. I will be waiting for you there."

That night in her sleeping hut, careful not to wake Den, Saba wept a little, for the children that she and Brychan would never have, for the winter nights that they would never lie warm under one rug, for all the things that they would never share together, and that she could never now share with anyone else; a little, too, for familiar and beloved things that she must leave behind, even for an old hound bitch of her father's, whom nobody would give bits of honeycake to, when she was gone.

But when the first light began to water the darkness, she got up and, moving very quietly because of Den, coiled up her hair and put on her silver bracelets that she only wore for best, then stepped out over the little slave lying in the doorway. She hoped that Cordaella would take Den and be good to her, and checked an instant, looking down, and saw that the child was awake and watching her. Den knew. But she would do nothing, tell nothing. They were a strange kind, the little Dark People.

She went on, out into the green dusk of the morning. She stole a barley loaf from the bake hut, and slipped out through a weak place that she knew of in the thorn hedge, and down toward the stream, and the willow tree above the ford.

Brychan was waiting for her. He did not ask if she was still sure. If she had not been, she would not have come. They took hands, and turned up the streamside. "I brought a loaf," Saba said. They had never eaten together. "At least we can share that. There might be wild strawberries."

It was a very gentle day; a sky watered between skim-milk blue and pale sweeps of cloud; a soft south wind blowing in from the sea, cool with the salt tang of it mingled with the sweetness of warm grass and thyme and the last of the elder blossom. They found their strawberries, and gathered them into a lap fold of Saba's skirt as they went along. Some of the berries, ripe, and crushed a little in the picking, stained the blue wool with flecks of purple. But that would not matter.

Presently they ate, among the hazel scrub where a little spring broke from the chalk, halving the loaf to the last crumb, and dividing the strawberries between them with meticulous care; and afterward drinking the cold hard water of the little spring from each other's cupped hands. Scarcely aware of what they did, they were making a small potent joining ceremony, out of the sharing of food and drink in the dapple shade under the alder branches.

Later, they wandered on again, still hand in hand like a pair of children. For a while they lay among the warm mousebrown of seeding grasses that the south wind swayed all one way. If you lifted your head, you could see the wind coming, laying the grass over in long silvery swaths. "When I was very young, I had a tame grass snake," Brychan said. "He went everywhere with me, hanging around my neck. He felt warm and dry, and he never made his bad white smell unless he was frightened; and he was never frightened when he was with me."

And Saba said, "The first thing that ever I can remember is lying in a soft rug beside the fire and watching my mother comb her hair. When she combed hard, it crackled and clung to the comb. I cannot have been more than two, because she died when I was two." And then she added, "Our mother."

And they were silent awhile, and then began again, wandering on once more and telling each other things as they went; exchanging thoughts and memories, as though they sought to share their whole lives and blend them into one, in the single day that was all they had.

Once they found themselves in the midst of a whole cloud of blue downland butterflies; once the shadow of a hawk fled over them. And at last, with the shadows beginning to lengthen, they turned downhill toward the woods.

"It has been a good day," Saba said.

"It has been a good day."

And now it was over. "Brychan, is it because we are sib, that we seem to be part of each other? Is it no more than that?" She cried it out suddenly frightened on the edge of the dark.

"You are sib to Garim, and to Cordaella. Full sib. This is another thing."

And she was reassured.

On the fringe of the woods, in a little hollow where hazel and elder crowded close as though to make them a sheltered resting place, they stopped, and sat down. There was bracken to shield them, and a shadow flush of willow herb among the trees, and somewhere a chiffchaff was calling as it flitted from branch to branch.

"Soon, they will come looking for us," Brychan said. "It is time to be on our way."

Saba nodded. "Show me the dagger again, first." And then, at something she saw in his eyes, "No, it is not that I am afraid."

"You need not be," he said. "We will be together, and I will not hurt you. No more than I hurt you when I got the bee sting out." And he pulled the dagger from his belt, and held it to her, laid across his palm. In the greenish shade, the three silver star lilies seemed to shine with a light of their own, as pale flowers do at twilight.

"It is beautiful," Saba said, as she had done before. "I am glad that it is beautiful."

They lay down together in each other's arms, and the bracken fronds closed over them.

# ABOUT THE AUTHORS

A. L. BARKER has been writing since the age of nine; her published career began in 1947 with *Innocents*, a collection of short stories which won the first Somerset Maugham Award. In 1962 she received a Cheltenham Festival Award in Literature. Her books include *The Joy Ride and After*, *A Case Examined*, and *Femina Real*.

Her story, "The Pleaser," was originally written for a magazine which ceased publication before the story was due to appear in print.

RUMER GODDEN was born in 1907 and spent most of her childhood in India. When she was twelve she and her three sisters were sent to school in England, but later she went back to India and has been going backward and forward ever since, perpetually homesick, she says, for one or the other. Her book *Two Under the Indian Sun*, written with her sister Jon, describes her childhood there. Her many novels are known the world over, have been translated into no less than fourteen languages, and several of them filmed. Her books include *The River*, *An Episode of Sparrows*, *The Greengage Summer*, and, most recently, *The Peacock Spring*, a novel which tells the story of an English teenager's love affair in modern Delhi.

Her story, "Fireworks for Elspeth," was first published in a collection of her short stories called *Swans and Turtles* (Macmillan, 1968), and also was the prototype for her novel *In This House of Brede*.

LYNNE REID BANKS was born in London; she spent the war years as an evacuee in the Canadian Prairies and her story, "Trust," written when she was eighteen, grew out of this experience. When she returned to England she studied acting at RADA; later she was one of the first women reporters for Independent Television News. Her first novel, *The L-Shaped Room*, became a bestseller and was later filmed. Among other books, she has written two novels, *Sarah and After* and *My Darling Villain*, for the Bodley Head's New Adult imprint.

This story, "Trust," has never been published before.

EMMA SMITH was only twenty-four when her first book, *Maidens' Trip*, was published in 1948. The story of three young girls working a pair of canal boats between London Docks and Birmingham, it was based on her own wartime experiences; *Maidens' Trip* won the John Llewelyn Rhys Memorial Prize and her next novel, *The Far Cry*, also won a prize, the James Tait Black.

Several years later, after she had married and then been widowed, she began to write novels for children, among them *Emily's Voyage* and *No Way of Telling*.

Emma Smith wrote "A Surplus of Lettuces" specially for this collection.

ROSEMARY SUTCLIFF says of her early life: "My schooling began late because of childhood illness, and ended when I was fourteen, owing to my entire lack of interest in being educated. But I showed signs of being able to paint and so from school I went to art school, trained hard, and eventually became a professional miniature painter." She switched to writing at the end of the last war, and is well known for her historical novels for children, among them *The Eagle of the Ninth* and *Warrior Scarlet*.

Her story, "Flowering Dagger," specially written for us and the first love story she has ever written, is set in the Bronze

Age, and the dagger is twin to a Mycenaean one in Athens Museum. This 1000 B.C. dagger has always fascinated her and she is delighted to give it a fictional home at last.

WILLIAM TREVOR was born in Cork, Ireland, in 1928, and educated at Trinity College, Dublin. He spent a great part of his life in Ireland, though he now lives in Devon, England. He began his career as a sculptor; his first novel, *The Old Boys*, was published in 1964 and won the Hawthornden Prize. His most recent novel, *The Children of Dynmouth*, which won the 1976 Whitbread Award, is about the pervading evil effect of a teenage boy on the people around him. William Trevor has also adapted many of his stories into highly successful television plays.

His story, "The Real Thing," was specially written for this collection.

PEGGY WOODFORD was born in India in 1937 where she spent her first nine years. She was educated in Guernsey, and at St. Anne's College, Oxford; then, after a year in Rome on a research scholarship, she did a variety of jobs from BBC TV research to sixth-form teaching. Her first novel, *Abraham's Legacy*, was published in 1963; her last two, *Please Don't Go* and *Backwater War*, were written for the Bodley Head's New Adult imprint. Her short story, "The Return," is in a sense a sequel to *Please Don't Go*.